Silence of the Hams

Also by Jill Churchill in Large Print:

Bell, Book, and Scandal
The House of Seven Mabels
It Had to Be You
Love for Sale
A Groom with a View
Someone to Watch over Me
War and Peas

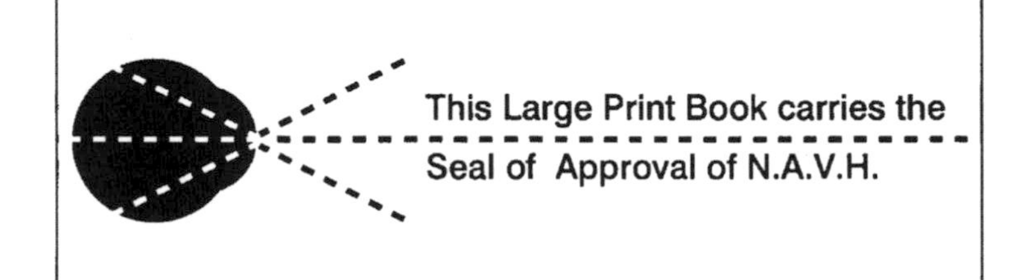

Silence of the Hams

A Jane Jeffry Mystery

Jill Churchill

This work is a novel. Any similarity to actual persons or events is purely coincidental.

Published in 2005 by arrangement with Avon books, an imprint of HarperCollins Publishers Inc.

Wheeler Large Print Cozy Mystery.

The text of this Large Print edition is unabridged. Other aspects of the book may vary from the original edition.

Set in 16 pt. Plantin by Elena Picard.

Printed in the United States on permanent paper.

Library of Congress Cataloging-in-Publication Data

Churchill, Jill, 1943–
Silence of the hams : a Jane Jeffry mystery / by Jill Churchill.
p. cm. — (Wheeler Publishing large print cozy mystery)
ISBN 1-58724-928-6 (lg. print : sc : alk. paper)
1. Jeffrey, Jane (Fictitious character) — Fiction. 2. Women detectives — Illinois — Chicago — Fiction. 3. Lawyers — Crimes against — Fiction. 4. Chicago (Ill.) — Fiction. 5. Single mothers — Fiction. 6. Suburban life — Fiction. 7. Large type books. I. Title. II. Wheeler large print cozy mystery.
PS3553.H85S55 2005
813′.54—dc22 2004028700

Silence of the Hams

National Association for Visually Handicapped
serving the partially seeing

As the Founder/CEO of NAVH, the only national health agency solely devoted to those who, although not totally blind, have an eye disease which could lead to serious visual impairment, I am pleased to recognize Thorndike Press* as one of the leading publishers in the large print field.

Founded in 1954 in San Francisco to prepare large print textbooks for partially seeing children, NAVH became the pioneer and standard setting agency in the preparation of large type.

Today, those publishers who meet our standards carry the prestigious "Seal of Approval" indicating high quality large print. We are delighted that Thorndike Press is one of the publishers whose titles meet these standards. We are also pleased to recognize the significant contribution Thorndike Press is making in this important and growing field.

Lorraine H. Marchi, L.H.D.
Founder/CEO
NAVH

* Thorndike Press encompasses the following imprints: Thorndike, Wheeler, Walker and Large Print Press.

– 1 –

The principal droned on, mispronouncing one name after another. Jane Jeffry glanced down at the program in her hand. Eleven-eighteenths of the way through, she estimated. Jane glanced at her best friend, Shelley, sitting next to her on the gym bleachers. Shelley had an amazing capacity for looking alert, whereas Jane was going to be black and blue tomorrow from pinching herself to stay awake.

She nudged Shelley, whose startled expression betrayed the fact that her mind had been miles away from the Chicago suburb high school where they were enduring awards night. Jane felt a little guilty about bringing Shelley back to reality. But only a little.

"Remind me again why we're doing this," Jane whispered.

"Because we were too stupid to read the directions on the birth control pill package?" Shelley suggested. "Because we thought babies were cute and didn't know this was ahead of us? Because we wanted to populate the world with little Jeffrys and Nowacks? Because —"

"Shelley! Get a grip!"

"Yes, yes. I'm sorry. It's just that this is the worst! I swear they rig this thing to give some idiotic award or another to every single child in the school. Look at this bunch! Best lap running times for every single gym class. There must be sixty of them! And the next batch is best Spanish accent in each class. Not best grade, mind you, best accent. That's for the poor little dolts who don't know a word of the language, but can roll their Rs. I approve of the idea of trying to make kids feel good about themselves, but why do I have to sit through it all? I'd rather spend two hours in the labor room!"

Jane had heard this tirade before. Had helped hone and polish it, in fact. She and Shelley each had a daughter doing this for the first time. Jane had another son graduating this year, but each of them also had a son starting junior high next year and were going to be serving another six-year sentence.

"No," Jane mused. "This is bad, but Halloween is the worst. Costumes," she said with a shudder. "And all that revolting candy that fires them up on sugar highs for a week. And then the thugs that come to the door to pillage and come back later to smash every pumpkin on the block. At least all our kids are old enough now to be past the costume stage."

A woman sitting behind them and eavesdropping leaned forward and said, "You don't really know about hell unless you have a child with a birthday on Christmas."

Jane and Shelley groaned in sympathy.

It was another hour before they escaped. "How did your husband get out of coming to this?" Jane asked as she joined the throng heading for the door.

"Oh, Paul's on a business trip."

"Wasn't he on a business trip the same week last year? And the year before?"

Shelley nodded. "Poor man doesn't think I notice how conveniently that works out for him. But he's afraid I might and he always brings home a really nice gift, just in case," she said. "Last year it was those diamond earrings," she said with a smile.

Finally it was over and they walked home, having determined that the closest parking places to the school were likely to be their own driveways anyway. It was a lush spring night. "As much pride as I take in being the most sedentary person in a four-state area, I'm glad you suggested walking," Jane said. "Only I feel like I should be running, just to get ahead on this week."

"That bad, huh?" Shelley leaned down and plucked a long blade of grass as they strolled along. She fitted it between her thumbs and blew on it fruitlessly. "I used to be able to make a killer noise that way," she said sadly.

Jane ignored this insight into her friend's history. "The last week of school is always hideous. Every team and club has a dinner or party, there are ghastly recitals and performances, these award things, and everything that's starting for the summer has a kickoff activity. It's the best argument I know for year-round school. And this year, of course, is Mike's graduation and the opening of the deli."

"The deli? Why does that involve you?"

"Me? It involves you, too. You promised!"

"I never!"

"You did. Remember last week when your battery died and I drove your car pool?"

Shelley muttered an obscenity. "I still don't see why we have to go to the grand opening of a deli. The opening of a dress shop, maybe, or a travel agency that's giving away a free trip to some island where there are no children allowed —"

"We're attending the deli opening because my firstborn has a summer job at the deli and it's motherly to rally around —"

"But I'm not Mike's mother," Shelley grumbled.

"— and mainly because Conrad and Sarah Baker are nice people who need all the support they can get."

"Oh-ho. Look out," Shelley said, pointing ahead of them on the sidewalk. A terribly fit, handsome man in his late forties was jogging toward them. He had one hand on his throat, apparently taking his pulse, and was looking at the watch on his other arm as he ran. He never did look up as he ran right between them.

"Excuse me?" Shelley called after him.

He turned, flashed a Hollywood-ish smile almost as showy and brilliant as his impressive prematurely white hair, and waved at them. It wasn't an apologetic wave, more of an acknowledgment of minions who had done well in staying out of his way.

At least, that was Jane's take. "He's a prize jerk," she said.

"Who was that?" a voice called out of the darkness.

Jane and Shelley detoured to join their neighbor Suzie, who was sitting on her front porch. Suzie Williams was a big woman, platinum blond and terribly frank. Jane thought of her as a nineties version of Mae West, but stunningly beautiful. Not only were they neighbors, but Suzie had a son the same grade as Jane's youngest and Shelley's boy. They'd all sat through a seemingly endless number of school plays, Cub Scout pack meetings, and summer softball and soccer games together.

"Are you sitting here in the dark trying to waylay men?" Jane asked Suzie, joining her on the porch.

"Worse things could happen," Suzie said with a dazzling smile. "So who was he?"

"You don't want to even consider it, Suzie," Shelley said. "He's Robert Stonecipher and he's a prize bastard."

"Stonecipher," Suzie mused. "I've heard of him, I think. An attorney, isn't he? Well, he might have enough money to take me away from the dizzying whirl of selling girdles for a living."

"Probably not," Jane said. "He's got a wife and, I hear, a girlfriend."

"A girlfriend?" Shelley asked. "Who?"

"My source didn't know," Jane answered.

"Oh, wait. He's the PCA, isn't he?" Suzie asked.

"PCA?"

"Politically Correct Asshole," Suzie said. "The one who's always trying to push weird stuff through the town council?"

"Right," Jane said. "Cat leash laws. No smoking anywhere, ever. Widening all the roads to provide running and biking lanes —"

"— four handicapped parking places at every place of business, twenty-mile-an-hour speed zones throughout the whole of the town —" Shelley added.

"— and full nutritional information on all restaurant menus," Suzie said. "I remember the slugfest over that one. If I wanted to eat healthy crap, which I don't, I'd stay home and fix it. Oh, and the crusade about the R-rated videos? He wanted to outlaw their rentals."

"You mean X-rated?" Shelley asked.

"No, I do not. There's all sorts of rules about X-rated. He wanted to make it a criminal offense to rent an R-rated movie. Jeez! If it weren't for R-rated movies, I'd have no sex life at all!"

"His latest effort was trying to shut down the Bakers' new deli," Jane said.

"Deli? Oh, that house at the end of the next block? How are they getting away with putting a business in a residential area anyway?" Suzie asked.

"Some quirk in the zoning laws," Jane said. "Mike told me about it. He's working as a delivery boy for them this summer, you know. Apparently the house was the first on the block — an old farmstead. During World War II the people who lived there had a big garden and raised chickens and sold vegetables and eggs at a roadside stand. I guess they were still doing it when the township was incorporated or whatever townships do and so there was a grandfather clause."

Shelley had sat down on the other side of Suzie and suddenly said, "Oh, yes! When I was a kid growing up here, my mother bought eggs from them. I'd completely forgotten that."

"I guess everybody had," Jane said. "When Conrad's wife and her sister inherited the house, they came back here to sell the place — did you know Conrad or Sarah, Shelley?"

"Only slightly. Conrad was two years ahead of me and Sarah was a year behind. Grace Axton — that's Sarah's sister — was in my class though."

"Anyway, Mike says Conrad did some research and discovered that the zoning had never been changed. It's something strange, like 'residential, with an exception to sell food products.' I mean, you couldn't put in a used car lot or anything."

"Conrad Baker figured this out himself?" Suzie asked. "I've run into him a couple times and I always thought he was pretty dim. Nice man, but about as bright as a breadstick."

Shelley said, "Oh, no. He's really bright. Just quiet. Back in high school he won all sorts of awards — in the days when awards really meant something. He went to college for two or three years, got in on the tail end of the hippie thing. He and Sarah got married right after she graduated and they went off to Oregon or someplace to be flower children. They ended up working in logging camps as cooks."

"How do you know all this stuff?" Jane asked, surprised, as she often was, by Shelley's memory for gossip. She supposed that came from having lived in the same place for so long. Jane had grown up a State Department brat, never living in one place for more than a year and often for less. When she married, she had been determined that her children would stay put and form the kind of lifelong friendships and connections that Shelley proved were possible.

"My mother was friends with Sarah and Grace's grandmother. Bridge club," Shelley explained.

"Seems to me that somebody mentioned the Bakers having lost a child, too," Suzie said.

"Yes, I've heard that, too," Shelley said. "But I don't know any of the details. One of my husband's sisters once missed a period and has carried on for years about her 'miscarriage' so I always take remarks like that with a grain of salt."

"Well, whatever their background, Conrad's certainly a good cook," Jane said. "He's been practicing for the opening and selling some of the stuff at cost to Mike. We had pastrami sandwiches last night that were fantastic. He's going to sell some of that trendy, healthy stuff — soyburgers and tofu chicken, which sounds revolting. But he's also got a gadget for making potato chips. Puts a little garlic seasoning in the oil and they're wonderful."

"Grease, salt, and starch. What more could a person ask?" Suzie said with a laugh. "So the handsome jogger was the one leading the fight against opening this heavenly place? Why would he care?"

"Because he paid far too much for his house and now he's trying to drag the neighborhood up to his standards?" Shelley said. "His wife, Rhonda, told me. They'd moved here from someplace in California and the price of the house looked great compared to California prices. It wasn't until they got moved in and were knee-deep in a lot of very expensive renovations that they realized they'd paid far too much. She didn't say so exactly, but suggested that he thought he could 'improve' the whole community and make his house worth what he paid. Having what he calls a 'market' in the middle of a residential area probably looks like a death knell to his plans."

"That, and he's just a natural-born grandstander, I think," Jane said. "Not only thinks he's superior to everyone else, but wants to make sure we all know it. I went to see him once and didn't like him at all."

"Went to see him? What do you mean?" Shelley asked.

"When my husband died I had to figure out how to handle the insurance money and Steve's portion of the profits from the family pharmacies, so I talked to a couple lawyers about setting up trusts for the kids' college expenses. Somebody suggested I consult the PCA, as Suzie so aptly calls him, so I did. He asked all sorts of questions — well, you'd expect that — but after a while I realized a lot of the questions weren't relevant. It took me a while. You know what a basket case I was for a while back then. By the time I realized what was going on, I'd blurted out all kinds of stuff about the pharmacies' finances, how much I'd invested myself back when I got that little inheritance and the business was having money problems, even the fact that the pharmacies had been having a long-running feud with the IRS about some deductions. I guess I thought he was just trying to be chummy and put me at my ease, or maybe trying to get a really complete view of the situation, but after a while, it started making me uneasy. He was asking about my relationship with my mother-in-law, about whom I said a few nasty things, I'm afraid. He even wanted to know who I inherited the money from, stuff like that."

"Why did he need to know that?" Shelley asked.

"I don't know. But it was creepy. And he was taking notes of everything I said. I quit pouring out personal information, asked a few questions, then got out of there," Jane said.

"But Jane, lots of people would love being asked all about themselves," Shelley said. "I'm always getting survey calls on the phone from people who are apparently amazed that I won't tell them my age and the family income. They whine about how the survey won't be valid without it, which leads me to think that other people are so flattered at being asked their opinions that they do give that information."

Jane laughed. "Little do the surveyors know that there are people who would happily pay you to keep your opinions to yourself. Like the school principal, the PTA president, the entire IRS, that police officer who tried to give you a parking ticket —"

Shelley sat up very straight. "That wasn't an opinion. It was a definition. Parking and standing are two distinctly different things and the officer agreed with me — eventually."

"Agreed? I heard he was weeping openly when you got through with him," Jane said.

Suzie laughed. "Here I am lurking in the dark, trying to catch a rich husband, and all I catch is the two of you! What a waste of a beautiful spring evening."

"So what did you decide about Mike's

graduation gift?" Shelley asked a little later.

Shelley and Jane had determined that after their ordeal they were richly entitled to a cup of coffee and a donut and were sitting at Jane's kitchen table, indulging. Jane's big yellow dog, Willard, was watching every bite either of them took, hoping for crumbs.

Jane leaned back and looked into the living room to make sure Mike wasn't there. "Oh, a car. I haven't got any choice. This is a delivery job he has this summer and Conrad can't afford to supply a vehicle. If Mike takes my car, I'm stranded. Katie's teaching at the Vacation Bible School and can walk, but Todd's got soccer team and guitar lessons, and I can't expect somebody else to drive him all the time. Mike will need a car for college anyway. He's determined to go to school in-state and come home often. I think he feels like I can't get along without him nearby."

"Can you?"

Jane laughed. "I'm not a complete incompetent even if I can't make policemen cry."

"I thought your mother-in-law had offered to get him a car," Shelley said.

"She didn't exactly offer. She dangled the possibility in front of me, but she was planning to get a new car herself and give him her old gray battleship of a Lincoln. He'd rather die than be seen driving an old-lady car like that, and I can't say that I blame him. So I convinced her I'd get him a car and she's getting him a computer instead."

"You can afford it, can't you? After all, you get Steve's third of the pharmacy profits and they seem to be doing well. Didn't they just open another one?"

"Yes, but I'm still putting half of it into the kids' college trusts, so my budget is pretty tight. The scary thing is, it's only three years until I face the same thing with Katie, and in the meantime my poor old station wagon will have to be replaced. It's practically an antique now."

Shelley shuddered. "Imagine our girls driving!"

Jane bit her tongue to keep from replying. If Denise turned out to be the same kind of driver her mother was, the neighborhood had a great deal to fear. Shelley's natural competitiveness reached its highest and worst point when she got behind the wheel of a car. The act of turning a key in the ignition triggered something wild and savage in her otherwise ladylike soul.

Shelley, guessing Jane's thoughts, grinned. "So what kind of car?"

"Uncle Jim's letting me know. He's been taking Mike with him, pretending he's looking for a car himself, and finding out what kinds Mike likes."

"But you're going to go buy it?"

Jane put her head in her hands. "I'm afraid so. I'm dreading it."

Shelley's eyes sparkled. "Oh, it could be fun."

"Fun? Are you crazy?"

Shelley grinned. "A feather in my cap. I've never made a car salesman cry. Yet."

— 2 —

The salesman didn't cry. But he didn't have much fun, either.

Jane's honorary Uncle Jim, a tough old Chicago cop who had been friends with her parents since before Jane was born, had reported that Mike's dream vehicle was a smallish black pickup truck. Though this hadn't crossed Jane's mind as a possibility, she quickly came to like the idea. It would allow her son to haul his belongings back and forth to college without involving her or her station wagon in long highway drives.

"Best of all, Shelley, there's no backseat," Jane told Shelley.

"What difference does that make?"

"Girls, Shelley. Girls and backseats can be a dangerous combination."

"Oh, right. Hormones and lust and dark nights on country roads. I'd almost forgotten all that."

On Shelley's orders, they stopped at the library and quickly copied a bunch of pages from various auto magazines and

Consumer Reports and piled back into Jane's car. Shelley skimmed the copied pages, crumpled and dog-eared them a bit, then laid them aside. "Aren't you going to read all that? Why did we copy it otherwise?"

"I read the one I needed to, the one about prices. The others are just to wave around and make it look like I've really studied the market and know what I'm doing," Shelley said confidently.

At first, the salesman was patronizing, calling them "ma'am," with a faint sneer. But after a few minutes with Shelley and her sheaf of papers, he became a little more respectful, switching to a state of vague alarm, and finally something that looked like panic. After twenty minutes, Shelley named a ridiculously low figure that she said was all they were prepared to pay. He laughed nervously, "I can't do that, ma'am."

"Well then, I'm sorry we've taken your time. Goodbye. Jane, put away your checkbook." She took Jane's elbow firmly and they headed back to where they'd parked the disgraceful station wagon down the street.

"But Shelley, it's exactly what he wants! Do we have to start all over again?" Jane whispered.

Shelley smiled. "No, we've won. You'll see."

They were only halfway to their car before the salesman caught up with them. He named a figure a hundred dollars over what Shelley had offered. She countered with fifty dollars less, and he caved in. Jane was dumbfounded.

Shelley drove Jane's car home, while Jane drove the new one to the county offices to get the tags and pay the taxes, then home, where she left it in Shelley's driveway. She'd called the insurance company and gotten the hideous news on what the additional premium would be and was casually loading the dishwasher a few minutes later when Mike and his best friend, Scott, got home from their last half day of school. Jane peeked while the boys circled the truck, admiring it.

"Hi, Mom," Mike said when they finally came in the house. "Whose truck is that?"

"Truck? I don't know." She went to the window again and looked. "Oh, that must be Shelley's nephew. She mentioned that he was coming by today."

The boys raved about it for a while and Jane went on cleaning the kitchen, trying not to grin. She tried to engage them in a discussion of how it felt to have finished high school, but the topic didn't interest them. Instead, they fixed Cokes for themselves and went back out to drool over the black pickup truck again. Jane followed.

"You really like this thing?" she asked innocently. She kicked a tire.

"Like it? Mom, it's the coolest thing on the road today," Mike said. "Just *look* at it!"

"I guess you'd like to have one," Jane said.

"Like one? Who wouldn't?"

Jane fished the keys out of her pocket. "Then why don't you take this one?"

Mike stared at the keys. Then looked at her. Then at the keys.

"You mean — ?"

Jane nodded. "It's yours."

Mike and Scott fell on each other, slapping, punching, and yelping. Mike grabbed Jane in a bear hug. "Jeez, Mom! Jeez! I can't believe it!"

Shelley had come out to join them when she heard the boys shouting. Scott was making a hideous yodeling noise while doing a victory dance around the truck and stopped to hug her. "Too cool! Too cool!" he crooned. "Mrs. J, you really came through," he said, mauling her in turn.

"We've gotta show the guys," Mike said, jingling the car keys.

"Don't forget the deli opening is in an hour," Jane warned.

Mike slapped his forehead. "Jeez!" he repeated. "Okay. Just a little drive then."

He and Scott got in the truck and sat for a few minutes, petting and caressing various parts of the interior and talking incomprehensible gibberish about the mechanics. Mike turned the key and they both made orgasmic noises as the engine revved to life. Mike hopped back out, gave his mother another hug and smack of a kiss, and asked if she wanted to ride along.

"No way, thanks. Don't forget your job."

The boys roared off and Jane watched until they were out of sight.

"Want a cup of coffee?" Shelley asked.

Jane sighed. "No, thanks. I believe I'll just go inside and have a good cry."

The old house Sarah Baker and her sister had inherited was spruced up and looking lovely. The clapboards had been repaired and painted a pristine white with shiny black shutters for accent. The old cement walk had been replaced with a wide brick one in an old-fashioned herringbone pattern and had a border of sweet-scented thyme along the edges. A martin house had pink morning glories twining their way up the post. The original wraparound porch at the front and sides had been enclosed with floor-to-ceiling crank-out windows, which were opened today.

Small white cafe tables for two and chairs with plump floral-patterned cushions were set up on the porch. At the center front of the house itself, one walked into what had once been a front hall, with a parlor and dining room to each side. The area had been opened up, and sparkling glass display cases enclosed an unbelievable array of deli foods. Jane assumed the back rooms of the first floor were kitchens and storage areas. There was no staircase visible, but Jane had heard that the second floor had been kept as living quarters. Conrad and Sarah Baker would be "living above the shop," as many small shopkeepers used to.

The decorating plan was in keeping with the Victorian house — lots of ferns and lush greenery — but everything was white and bright and clean instead of characterized by the dark sobriety that had been fashionable when the house was new. Jane and Shelley had arrived early, but so had many other curious neighbors. Nearly all the little tables on the porch were occupied by people sampling Conrad's cooking when Jane and Shelley arrived. Conrad, in a chef's white jacket and hat, greeted them with a tray. "Ladies, how good of you to come!" he said heartily. "Have a seat or roam around as you like."

Conrad was a large, florid-faced man who obviously enjoyed eating as much as cooking. He wasn't fat, just big and fairly solid-looking, as ex-football players often get in middle age. His wife, Sarah, was behind him, passing out plates and silverware. She was a small, thin woman with tiny, delicate features and a mop of curly dark blond hair held back with clear plastic combs. She had a shy, quiet manner, and though she was smiling, she looked as if this sort of mingling was painful.

Shelley introduced herself and Jane to Sarah Baker, who said softly, "Oh, I remember you from school days, Shelley. And I've talked to Jane on the phone a couple times. Thanks for coming. If you'd like to sit down while there's still a place to, I could bring you some of our special tea, and Conrad will be back around with sandwiches."

Jane, whose motto was "Never pass up a chance to sit down," took her up on the offer. The tea, when it arrived, was a very nice Earl Grey with the merest hint of a floral scent they couldn't identify. "I may never cook again," Jane said, sampling a cucumber dip Conrad had brought around with tiny sandwiches, some of his homemade potato chips, and a generous serving of cherry crisp.

"Delicious," Shelley said around a mouthful of salmon mousse.

A tall woman who looked like an elongated version of Sarah Baker stopped at the table. "Shelley, nice to see you," she said.

"Grace Axton, this is my friend Jane Jeffry. Jane is Mike's mother."

"I'm glad to meet anyone who could raise such a great kid," Grace said. "We can already tell it's going to be nearly impossible to replace him when he goes to college in the fall. In his new truck! He's so proud of it."

"Mike's here?" Jane asked. In the dark, most motherly recesses of her mind, she'd been half afraid he'd forgotten everything in his thraldom with the vehicle.

"In the back, helping with cleanup before he starts deliveries. Have you seen the kitchens?"

"No, we didn't know we could," Shelley replied.

"Sure. We're anxious to show off everything."

Shelley said, "Grace, I hardly recognized Sarah. I mean, she looks the same, but I remembered her being really bubbly and outgoing."

"People change," Grace Axton said shortly, and added with a laugh, "I didn't used to have a neck like a chicken, either, but we're not in high school anymore."

"You have a perfectly fine neck," Shelley objected, "but if you saw the back of my upper arms —" After a few chummy, if depressing, comments about aging and the exchange of the names of a couple plastic surgeons, Grace moved off to greet other newcomers.

Mike stopped by to thank Jane again for the truck, then, carrying a cardboard box full of paper bags and cartons, went on his first delivery. As he went down the sidewalk, Shelley murmured, "I can't believe it. Look who's coming."

"What a hell of a nerve," Jane agreed as Robert Stonecipher stepped in the door and glanced around critically. With his showy white hair and handsome features, he looked as if he had been designed as part of the decor. Or he would have, had he not been scowling.

"And he's got his pet dog with him," Shelley added, glaring at the sour-looking old man who was right behind Stonecipher.

"Who's that?"

"I can't think of his name. I always want to call him Foster Brooks," Shelley said. "Foster Hanlon, that's it. He's been hopping up and down and talking ugly about the deli opening, too."

"But they've lost the battle. Why would they show up for the opening? You'd think they'd be embarrassed to visit the site of their defeat. Who's the woman with them?" Jane asked, eyeing the newcomer. She was not especially young, but was one of those terribly "fresh" people who always look as if they'd just stepped out of a tepid shower and a brisk rubdown with something organic that was awfully expensive and environmentally sound.

"Oh, you know her, Jane. That Emma person who taught the aerobics class we took. Emma Weyworth — no, Weyrich."

Jane shuddered at the memory. In a rare fit of healthiness, Shelley had insisted that the two of them shape up and had enrolled them in the class at the community center. They lasted fifteen minutes. When the instructor called for a short break, they gathered their belongings and crept away. But Emma had seen their break for freedom and followed them to the parking lot to try to drag them back with a lot of what Jane considered highly personal and insulting remarks about how much they both needed to improve their bodies.

"It figures she'd be hanging out with Stonecipher," Jane said. "Health nuts, both of them."

"I think she's his secretary as well," Shelley said. "Or a paralegal or something."

The threesome entered the house and Jane and Shelley went back to sampling and reviewing the food they'd been served.

They visited with a few other neighbors, some of whom had vaguely (and silently) opposed the deli, but had been won over by the quality of the food and the decorating. "It really doesn't look like a business," one said grudgingly. "I was afraid it was going to be a real blight. But except for the sign out front, you'd think it was just a well-kept old house. It must have cost a fortune to renovate it. I hear it was Grace Axton's money. I don't imagine the Bakers came back here with a pot to pee in."

Conrad was circulating with another tray of goodies, to which Jane and Shelley shamelessly helped themselves. The deli was becoming more crowded by the minute, and they finally, reluctantly, gave up their places at the small table, leaving a humiliating pile of crumbs.

"It looks like we rubbed our food in instead of eating it," Jane whispered.

"Let's peek at the kitchen before we leave," Shelley said, nearly tripping over a toddler in her haste to distance herself from the scene of culinary devastation.

It was a kitchen to die for. Vast white countertops, steel sinks, two brushed-chrome fronted dishwashers, and every imaginable appliance. Around the soffit hung an array of copper utensils that made Jane's mouth water, even though she knew she'd hate having to clean them. Today the food was being served on plastic plates because of the crush, but in the future the serving dishes would be the oval green plates that were stacked in the open cabinets. The serving dishes alone represented a mind-boggling financial investment.

After admiring everything, Jane said, "I'll meet you outside. I have to find a bathroom."

"Just down that hallway," Grace Axton said, entering the kitchen and catching Jane's words.

Jane followed Grace's directions. While she was washing her hands, she heard a crash. By the time she'd dried her hands and disposed of the paper towel, she could hear someone screaming. She stepped out of the bathroom.

A crowd of people was descending on an open doorway along the hallway between the bathroom and the kitchen. As she neared the door, someone shoved a sobbing Sarah Baker out of the doorway and into her arms.

"Sarah! What's wrong!"

Sarah was blubbering. "He's dead! Oh, my God —"

"Dead? Who's dead?" Jane asked, fearing the answer was Conrad.

Grace Axton pushed through the crowd and grabbed at Sarah. "Honey, come away from here. Come on."

Somebody behind her gave a push and Jane found herself, against her will, in the room where somebody was dead. It was a storage room, as bright and clean as the rest of the deli. Cardboard cartons were neatly stacked on shelving that ran clear around the room except for the doorway where she stood and another doorway on the outside wall. A large chrome rack was lying on the floor. It had held hams, which had rolled all over the floor. Lying in the midst of the hams was a facedown figure. But nobody needed to see the face to know who it was. The showy, snowy white hair could only belong to Robert Stonecipher.

— 3 —

Everybody in the hallway seemed to want in the room.

Jane wanted out.

Pushing her way gently but firmly, she struggled into the hall and through the kitchen and sales area. She found Shelley waiting outside.

"What on earth's happening?" Shelley said. They could hear the wail of sirens, and the people still in the deli were standing around in worried knots.

Shaken, Jane explained. "There was a big metal rack in the middle of the storage room that apparently fell over on Robert Stonecipher. It's a madhouse in there."

"Was he hurt?"

"I think he's dead, but I didn't get close enough to find out. Sarah Baker was crying and saying he was dead. I don't know —"

"Storeroom?"

"Between the kitchen and the bathroom. I heard the crash."

"Poor Conrad and Sarah," Shelley said.

"Stonecipher was an obnoxious bastard, but I wouldn't wish that on him. Still, if he had to get himself killed or injured, why did it have to be here? And today, to wreck their grand opening? As if he hadn't already given them enough trouble on purpose."

An ambulance pulled up in front of the deli. Shelley and Jane stepped onto the lawn so they wouldn't be in the way of the emergency staff who leaped out and ran into the building carrying complicated equipment.

"Let's get out of here," Jane said. "We can't be any help and I hate to stand around being a gawker."

They walked home, and Jane spent a depressing hour paying bills and tidying her small basement office. And trying very hard not to think about that sprawled figure lying half under the rack. What could have made it fall over? It looked as if it had been freestanding in the middle of the room, but surely something that large and heavy-looking doesn't spontaneously topple over simply because somebody walks by it. Suppose it had been Mike in the room when it went over! Her heart went cold. No, she couldn't bear to think about it.

Instead, she looked longingly at the pile

of paper sitting next to her computer. For nearly a year now she'd been working on what she called her "story." She was afraid to call it a book for fear that such a weighty word would get in the way of her ever finishing it. And, too, if it was a book, she'd have to think about what to do with it if and when she ever finished. Instead, she puttered with the story, enjoying the adventure of spending a few hours every week with a character she'd made up and enjoyed having adventures with. It had begun when she'd taken a "Writing Your Life Story" class with her mother the previous summer. Jane hadn't wanted to write her own story — she only took the class to do something with her mother during her visit — so she invented Priscilla and started telling her story instead.

Now Priscilla, a woman of the eighteenth century who'd lived a long and exciting life, had become a friend, and Jane found herself wishing she could turn on the computer and spend the rest of the day with her. Instead, real life called.

Jane ran a comb through her hair, spent a few frantic moments searching for her car keys, then drove to the grade school to face the horror of the last day of school. The kids would explode from the doors in a few minutes in that state of high-pitched hysteria that made her nerves fray. In two days they'd be moping around asking what there was to do, but today they'd be wound as tight as tops at the prospect of the whole glorious summer vacation stretching before them.

Jane had forgotten to bring a book to read, so while she waited, she thought about the accident at the deli. As callous as Shelley's comments might have sounded to an outsider, Jane agreed with them. Robert Stonecipher had meant nothing to her. He was a bully — and a pious bully at that, the worst sort. But if he had really died when the rack of hams fell on him, it would forever blot what should have been a fine, glorious day for the Bakers and Sarah's sister, Grace. They seemed to be nice, hardworking people, and it was a pity that their grand opening should be marred by something so terrible.

There was a muffled sound of a buzzer, then the parking lot of the grade school was suddenly full of children — screaming, jumping, overwrought children. Many of them, including her son and Shelley's, carrying paper bags full of school papers and supplies that would clutter their rooms for months and finally be discarded only when school started again in the fall. Three months, Jane thought dismally.

Summer vacation meant ear infections from swimming; fights about curfews; slumber parties in the middle of the week; ravening hordes of children eating, as a mid-afternoon snack, the one absolutely essential ingredient of the dinner she had planned and not even telling her. Summer was wet swimming suits left on beds and wasp stings.

On the other hand, summer also meant real tomatoes at roadside stands instead of the mealy imitations in the grocery store. No math papers to help with. Sleeping with the windows wide open and waking up to the sound of birds instead of the alarm clock. No hideous heating bills or snow shoveling or money spent dry cleaning sweaters. Yes, summer had its compensations.

She scooped the boys up, took them home to change clothes and have a snack, then drove them and Shelley to the first soccer practice of the season with the new coach. Their former coach had moved away and the new volunteer was a very good-looking man who introduced himself to the kids and parents as Tony Belton. Normally Shelley and Jane dropped the boys off for practice and fetched them later, but with a new coach, it was de rigueur to sit through at least one practice.

Tony Belton was thirty-ish and had soccer-player legs that looked extremely good in shorts. There was a romantic, European look about him. He had dark curly hair, black eyelashes, and startlingly light blue eyes. He was also very personable, and talked a bit about how much soccer had meant to him as a kid and the values of learning teamwork. It was the same sort of rah-rah stuff coaches always spouted, but coming from him, it seemed fresh and sincere.

"Isn't it wonderful of him to have had this session today?" a woman sitting next to Jane and Shelley said as Tony Belton and the boys took to the field.

"Wonderful," Jane said, perplexed. "But why today especially?"

"Well, his partner died just a few hours ago. I imagine he's devastated."

"His partner?" Shelley asked.

"Robert Stonecipher. You know, that lawyer who's always starting trouble."

"He really did die?" Jane asked.

The woman nodded. "Killed by a rack of hams that fell over on him at the deli opening. It sounds so silly."

"I know. We were there when it happened," Jane said. "So Tony Belton is his law partner?"

She and Shelley exchanged a quick glance that said Tony Belton was either a very good actor, or he *wasn't* exactly devastated by his partner's death.

Soccer practice was mercifully short because the grade school graduation was that night. When they arrived home, Mike had his new truck in the driveway showing it off to Jane's daughter Katie and her friend Jenny.

"Way cool, Mom!" Katie cooed.

Jane knew exactly what this meant: that Katie considered Mike's graduation present a precedent to be met in two years when she graduated. This was something Jane had considered — but apparently not seriously enough.

"It is *not* a graduation present, Katie. It's because Mike needed it for his job." But Katie's grin at this disclaimer said it all. She'd have a delivery job, too, when the time came. Jane patted the hood of the station wagon and said, "Pull yourself together, old dear. We're in this together for life." She added, "Mike, why are you here instead of working?"

"I was delivering dinner to Mrs. Williams and saw Katie in the yard. I'm off. Oh, by the way, Mom, Mrs. Baker's in the hospital."

"Oh, no! What happened to her?"

Mike came over to talk to her quietly without his siblings listening. "She went to pieces about that guy dying. I mean, it was awful and I'm glad I wasn't there, but she just went bonkers and they took her away, too. Just thought you might want to know. You going to the twerp's graduation tonight? That's kinda dumb, a grade school graduation."

"You didn't think so when it was yours," Jane said.

"Sure I did. I just went along with it for your sake," Mike said with a grin. "See you later. Scott and I are going out after work to show off The Beast."

"Don't be late. Tomorrow's going to be a long day. Remember, you have to be up early to pick up your cap and gown."

Mike had to practically peel his younger brother and sister off his new truck before he could get away.

Jane threw together a quick dinner and hastily sewed a button on the shirt Todd was wearing that evening. Thanks to a revolt among the parents two years earlier, the boys no longer had to wear expensive little suits they'd outgrow in two weeks for the grade school commencement, as they had when Mike graduated. The girls still insisted on dressing like princesses, but the boys only had to be forced into button-up shirts and ties.

The ceremony, Jane had to admit, was charming. Partly because it didn't have any genuine significance like a high school graduation, and also because the school principal didn't appear to take it terribly seriously. It was more of a party atmosphere than a mock-serious occasion. There was a processional — nobody had figured out a way to avoid that — and a mercifully short speech by the principal, then a couple upbeat songs by the chorus and the awarding of certificates of graduation. It was over in just under forty-five minutes. And that included the punch and cookies afterward.

"Wow, that was almost painless," Shelley said as they walked back to the car. Their boys trailed behind them. "Well, except for your mother-in-law being there."

Thelma Jeffry had insisted on trying to treat it as a maudlin occasion, but Shelley and Jane had both been so relentlessly cheerful that she couldn't carry it off. "Just wait until tomorrow if you think she was bad tonight," Jane said. "Mike is the first grandchild to graduate from high school. She'll pull out all the stops."

"I told you to lie about the date," Shelley said.

Jane laughed. "I couldn't talk the printer into faking a separate announcement."

"There's probably a black market. You just didn't try hard enough."

When they got home, Katie reported curtly that Mel VanDyne had called and left a message that he'd like to come by later in the evening if it was convenient. Mel was what Katie referred to archly as Jane's "significant other" since she felt it was undignified for her mother to have a "boyfriend." Especially since she didn't have a boyfriend of her own.

Mel was also a police detective, and Katie's version of his message sounded official.

"Wonder what he wants?" Jane asked. "He was supposed to be on duty tonight so he can help me chaperone the all-night high school party tomorrow."

"What a fun date you are," Shelley said.

"Coffee?" Jane asked.

"Oh, maybe half a cup. Was that an expression of disapproval?" she added, gesturing toward the door Katie'd gone through.

Jane nodded. "It comes and goes. She likes Mel. She doesn't like *me* and Mel. She was still Daddy's little girl when Steve died, and she goes through spells of idolizing him and thinking, like Thelma does, that I should have gone into permanent mourning."

"It's just her hormones," Shelley said. "If it weren't that, it would be something else. Denise has decided that I willfully and deliberately passed on my straight-hair genes to her."

"She's right, isn't she?" Jane said, grinning as she plugged in the coffeemaker.

"Of course she is. And wait till she sees what happens to her thighs when she turns thirty if she thinks straight hair is bad."

They were both on their second cup of coffee and happily rummaging through a furniture catalog when Mel arrived.

"This isn't the visit where you say you can't help chaperone and I have to rip out your throat, is it?" Jane greeted him.

"No — not quite. This is an official visit."

"Not the parking ticket!" Shelley exclaimed. "The officer said —"

He held up both hands. "No, I just need some information."

Jane supplied him with coffee and put a plate of sugar cookies on the coffee table in the living room. "Don't even think about it, Willard," she said sternly to the big yellow dog who shambled out of the dining room when he heard the plate being set down. Willard sprawled on the floor at Mel's feet and gazed up at him soulfully.

"You two were at the opening of the deli at the end of the next block this afternoon, weren't you?"

Mel was a few years younger than Jane, which always made her slightly uncomfortable, but today he looked tired and annoyed and not quite so young.

"We were. Unfortunately," Shelley answered.

"I wonder if you could each make a list of everybody you remember seeing there and approximate times. And then I'll need to know which of those people had any connection with Robert Stonecipher that you know of."

"Mel, what's this about?" Jane asked. "It was just an accident and —"

"Jane, somebody else said they saw you in the storeroom after it happened."

She nodded. "I was, for a second."

"And you saw that rack?"

"The one with the hams that fell over? Yes, of course."

"Did you notice the base of it? The legs?"

"I didn't pay any attention," Jane replied.

Mel sighed. "Well, if you had, you'd have realized right away that it couldn't possibly fall over by itself. It had to be pushed. Hard."

"Somebody killed Stonecipher?" Jane exclaimed.

"It sure looks like it," Mel said grimly.

— 4 —

"Mike!" Jane exclaimed. "He can't go back there!"

"What?" Mel asked, disconcerted by the sudden shift in the conversation.

"My son *cannot* work where somebody is killing people!"

"Hold it, Jane. We have no idea yet what really happened. Someone may have pushed it over without knowing he was behind it or —"

"It doesn't matter."

"Look, Jane, I think you should just cool down a little before you make a snap decision," he said warily.

"Mel's right," Shelley said. "Besides everything else, Stonecipher was a jerk who probably had more enemies than we could guess. Even if someone did kill him, that doesn't mean they'd harm anybody else."

"Jane —" Mel said hesitantly, "you know I'd never butt in on your mothering and I'm not now, but I was once an eighteen-year-old boy myself." He paused, waiting to see how this was going over. When Jane merely stared back at him, he went on, "Boys that age are awfully sensitive about having their mothers tell them what to do. And Mike's a sensible, responsible kid, which would make it even harder for him to take being treated like a child."

Shelley backed him up. "Jane, I'd feel just like you do, but Mel has a point. Mike thinks he's the one who takes care of you. To be told *you've* decided he has to quit his job would be really tough on him."

"Not as tough as getting killed," Jane said.

"Jane, think about it," Shelley said. "If some madman killed Stonecipher at random, he's unlikely to keep coming back to the deli. And Mike's hardly ever there anyway except to pick up orders to deliver. It's not as if he's the night watchman or anything. And if Stonecipher was killed by somebody who meant to go after him specifically, Mike's in no danger in that case either."

Jane shook her head. "My brain knows you're both right, but my heart doesn't agree."

Mel, having given his one piece of advice, waited patiently. Shelley said, "If you want my advice — and even if you don't —

I think you ought to tell Mike how you feel, but leave the decision up to him. That's how you always operate with him."

"But it's too late for him to get another job for the summer, and you know kids his age have no sense of their own mortality," Jane objected.

"But he cares a lot for your welfare, Janey," Mel said. "And as the investigating officer in this matter, I have to say I don't believe he's in any danger. No more than we're all in, all the time."

"Just consider it, Jane," Shelley put in.

"Okay, okay. I'll think about it before I say anything." She took a deep breath and said, "All right, Mel. What did you want of us? Neither of us saw anything happen."

"Yes, but you saw who was there. Would you both write down everybody you can remember, then we'll talk about your lists."

Jane went to the desk and took out two legal pads she used for taking phone messages. She and Shelley separately composed their lists, asking occasional questions of each other. "What's the name of that woman with the weird apricot-colored hair?" "Who's that guy who always wears the checked flannel shirts?" "Did I really see Milly Vogrin or do I just think I did because I see her everywhere?"

Finally, when they'd written down all the names they knew, Mel copied it onto one list, eliminating duplicates, and started going through it name by name.

"To your knowledge, do any of these people have any connection to Robert Stonecipher?"

To the first couple names, both women shook their heads helplessly.

"What about Charles and LeAnne Doherty," Mel asked, working his way down the list.

"He was LeAnne's attorney when they got divorced," Shelley said.

"Divorced? But they were there together?" Mel asked.

"They remarried."

"Oh, my gosh!" Jane exclaimed. "Stonecipher was her attorney?"

"What's so surprising about that?" Mel asked.

"I guess it shouldn't be a surprise. It's just that LeAnne never mentioned his name. She just called him — well, never mind. You see, they got divorced and LeAnne just picked somebody out of the phone book to represent her. And he absolutely cleaned Charles out. Left him virtually broke. LeAnne was real pissed and didn't care."

"Wait — how do you know this?" Mel asked.

She told me, of course," Jane said. "We were room mothers together last year. So her attorney — Stonecipher as it now turns out — wrung Charles dry. But when all the dust had settled, LeAnne discovered that she only got a pittance. Everything had disappeared into legal fees. She even went to another lawyer to try to recover some of it, and he pretty much told her she'd been a dummy. Anyhow, it created a weird kind of bond between her and Charles and they eventually got back together. They went to marriage therapy and so on and got married all over again. Which was great for them, but they hardly had anything left to live on. They had to declare bankruptcy and start over. Charles had worked for a bank or a mortgage company or something like that."

"Euuw," Shelley put in. "Companies like that aren't wild about bankrupt employees."

"Right. He lost his job and they both had to work like dogs to get back up to speed. They finally got enough saved to open that little cubbyhole dry cleaners next to the grocery store."

"I'd never heard this story," Shelley said

somewhat resentfully. "I knew about the divorce and remarriage, but not the rest of it. I only knew Stonecipher was her lawyer because somebody at the bake sale was asking about divorce attorneys, and she said he'd represented her and she warned everybody to stay away from him."

"Was she angry when she said that?" Mel asked.

Jane and Shelley realized at the same instant that they'd been making a case against the Dohertys. "No, no!" Shelley said hastily. "More wry and embarrassed than angry. It was a couple years ago and they've got it together now and I'm sure —"

Jane put her hand over her mouth.

"What?" Mel asked.

"Nothing."

"Janey," he said sternly.

"Well, you'll find out anyway, I guess. I was reading that little 'good news' newspaper/shopper thing we usually let turn to mulch in the driveway last week and saw something about the city council meeting. Apparently Stonecipher was threatening a lawsuit against a dry cleaners. Something about hazardous chemicals. I don't think the article mentioned which one it was, but it could have been the Dohertys."

"I'll check it out," Mel said. "So they

were both there at the deli opening?"

"I'm the one who saw them," Shelley said, closing her eyes to picture it. "But I'm not positive I saw both of them. It's just that they usually do go everywhere together. I know I saw LeAnne because she had on that navy and white sweater I tried to get you to buy, Jane. Remember, I told you if you waited for it to go on sale you'd miss your chance?"

Mel cleared his throat.

"Well," Shelley huffed, "LeAnne was there, but I'm not sure about Charles."

Mel went back to the list. "I understand both Stonecipher and a man named Foster Hanlon were trying to get the deli shut down, and Hanlon was there as well."

"They came together," Jane said. "Well, at about the same time, anyway. But Hanlon was on Stonecipher's side of the dispute."

"As far as we know," Shelley said ominously.

"What do you mean?" Mel asked.

"Just that sometimes generals disagree with each other," Shelley said. "They were both almost professional troublemakers. Maybe Stonecipher took the lead and Hanlon didn't like the way he handled it and blamed Stonecipher for losing the battle."

"Shelley, that's crazy," Jane said. "Killing somebody over a zoning ordinance?"

"Killing somebody over *anything* is crazy," Shelley reminded her. "And it could have been accidental. Suppose they got into a shouting match in the storage room and Hanlon got so furious he wanted to take a shot at Stonecipher and angrily shoved at the rack instead?"

Jane made a so-so motion with her hand. "Maybe. Except I don't think there was a shouting match. I was in the bathroom and heard the crash and I hadn't heard yelling before that."

"Well, a hissing match, then," Shelley persisted.

"You'd really like it to be Hanlon, huh?" Jane said, smiling.

"I wouldn't mind. Remember when I was on that planning committee for the well-baby clinic and he made such a nasty flap?"

"Only vaguely."

"He was certain that what he called 'riff-raff' was going to descend on us like locusts. To hear him tell it, wild-eyed pinko liberals were going to hire buses to gather up mothers and children from the streets of inner-city Chicago and bring them out here for free treatment." Shelley paused.

"Which sounded like a pretty good idea to me, actually. There was a strong odor of bigotry about the whole thing. Ugh. Nasty man," she said, shuddering elaborately.

Jane thought for a minute. "You know, it would be killing two birds with one stone, so to speak, if he'd gotten mad enough at Stonecipher to kill him. What better place to do it than the deli? A murder at the deli might also hurt Conrad's business enough to shut him down."

"I think we're wandering pretty far afield here," Mel said. "Could we go back to the list, please?"

They filled Mel in on Conrad, Sarah, and Grace. "I think Grace is a partner in the business," Shelley said. "She talked about 'we' and 'us' and 'our' business. I got the impression that she actually invested more than just her share of the house she and Sarah inherited. But it's only my impression. It must have cost a fortune for the renovations, the equipment, the supplies, not to mention that there must have been legal fees to defend themselves against Stonecipher and Hanlon trying to close them down. But as far as making them suspects in his death — well, it's the opposite, really. They'd won the battle."

Mel made a note and said, "Now, it seems that Stonecipher's business associates were there, too. What about Emma Weyrich?"

Jane and Shelley told him a whole lot more than he wanted to know about the aerobics class.

"But do you know anything about her relationship with her employer?" he asked, cutting them off.

Not a thing, they admitted.

"But she came to the deli with him?"

"She and Hanlon both followed him in the door," Jane said. "But I don't know if they actually came together."

"And his law partner? Tony Belton?"

"Tony Belton was there?" Shelley asked. "I didn't see him."

"He was there when I arrived," Mel said. "Do you know him?"

"He's the boys' new soccer coach. We met him at the practice later in the afternoon," Shelley said. "But he's a handsome man. I think we would have noticed him if he'd been at the deli when we were." At his questioning look, Shelley smiled and added, "Just because I'm married doesn't mean I'm blind, does it?"

"What about Rhonda Stonecipher, the deceased's wife?"

"I know her, but I didn't see her there," Shelley said. "Was she?"

Mel nodded. "What's she like?"

Jane answered. "Middle-aged, tummy-tucked, beauty-shopped, nail-saloned. And stingy as hell. I was on a committee with her once — to raise money to replace the playground equipment at the park. She insisted that we have our first meeting at a very expensive restaurant. Everybody thought it was nice of her to treat us to lunch, but then we found that we not only had to pay for our own lunches, we had to pay for hers, too, because she 'forgot' her credit card. Nobody believed it, but then she got us a second time. After one of the meetings we all went out for dessert and suddenly she had to leave only seconds before the bill came."

"Sounds like a match made in heaven," Mel said.

"Not really," Shelley put in. "Rhonda stiffed me for a lunch once, too, but she's so pleasant about it. She's one of those people who make you feel like you're her best friend when you're talking to her. Very chirpy and cheerful and chummy."

Jane nodded. "That's true. And with the park thing, she was a good worker. She had some great ideas and managed to extract a lot of money from people. I guess practice makes perfect."

"I don't suppose there's any hope that you two could tell me exactly when you saw any of the people you did see?" Mel asked.

"None at all," Jane replied. "We were there for the food, not as witnesses."

Jane couldn't get to sleep that night. Mike was still out, and she kept listening for him to come home, while telling herself she was being obsessive. In a few months he'd be away at college and she'd never know what time he was coming in. But, as her own mother had frequently told her, "Motherhood is an incurable disease." She reminded herself she had no reason to worry about Mike. Of all her children — of all the children she knew well, in fact — he was the most sensible and responsible. A smart aleck, of course, but sensible just the same. While Katie and Todd threw fits about her rules and restrictions, Mike never had. He just made fun of her.

"Oh, yeah, Mom," he'd said cheerfully when she set his curfew at eleven a few years ago, "I forgot that the knife-wielding mass murderers all have their alarms set for eleven." Laughing in spite of herself, she'd backed off and settled for eleven-thirty.

She knew he wasn't out drinking, or driving like a loony, or letting anyone else drive his new truck. But she still worried. She knew it was partly because of the death at the deli, but on reflection she knew both Mel and Shelley were right. And she was oddly comforted by learning that both Stonecipher's wife and his partner had been there, too. Surely the reason for his death had something to do with his life. And nothing whatsoever to do with Mike or anybody else.

She finally fell into a light sleep, but woke again soon. There was an odd noise somewhere. Staggering to the bathroom, she realized the plumbing was making that sound that meant water was running somewhere. But she hadn't left the dishwasher or yard sprinkler running, so what was it? Dear God, what if the antique water heater had finally crumbled. How did a person find a plumber, much less afford one in the middle of the night!

She threw on her robe and hurried down the stairs, but as she passed through the kitchen, she heard a noise in the driveway. Thank God. Mike was home. Men, even young ones, had some built-in genetic affinity with pipes.

She glanced out the kitchen window and

found herself tearing up again. Mike was home, all right. And she'd remember what she was seeing now every time she made a car payment.

It was one in the morning and he was washing his new truck as tenderly as a mother washes a newborn.

— 5 —

Jane got up early, took her coffee outside, and sat on the patio. Her cats, Max and Meow, assumed, erroneously, that this activity was going to have something to do with food for them, and followed her, stropping themselves against her legs. "You were just fed!" she reminded them. Willard wanted to go bark aimlessly and she wouldn't let him, so he settled next to her and mumbled to himself about every bird and squirrel he saw. A few minutes later Todd stumbled out to sit with her. Not being a teenager quite yet, he hadn't adopted the belief that summers were for sleeping till noon and staying up all night.

Fortunately, he wasn't gabby in the morning, so they sat in companionable silence, Jane with her coffee, Todd with a glass of milk. Todd petted Willard with his foot, and the big dog rolled over, waving his saucer-sized feet in the air and groaning happily.

Mike joined them shortly. He looked

tired, but happy. "I'm going to go get my cap and gown and come back to sleep until I have to go to work at eleven," he said.

"About your job —" Jane began.

"Todd, Willard needs a few Frisbee tosses before I go," Mike said. "You know where it is?"

Todd got up and went back in the house and Mike sat down. "Look, Mom, I know everything you're going to say. Somebody got killed at the deli —"

"You knew that?"

"It's what everybody's saying. Mel and a couple other cops are talking to everyone who was there and that doesn't happen for an accident. Anyway, you don't think it's safe. But, Mom, I can't quit. Mr. Baker's counting on me to do the deliveries. His wife's in the hospital and Mrs. Axton has to do double work to help with the cooking, which she's not very good at, and the cleaning up, and I can't leave them in a lurch like that. But I'll make you a deal. I'll only go inside to pick up stuff to deliver. If it's not ready, I'll wait outside. I really should be helping in the kitchen and stuff, but I won't if it'll keep you off my back about it."

"That's a deal," Jane agreed, knowing he'd keep his end of the bargain and vowing that she would, too.

Todd came back with the Frisbee and Mike flung it for the dog a couple times before he left. "So what's up for the day, Todd, old thing?" Jane asked.

"Taking my Legos over to Elliot's. He's got a book of things you can build and there's this neat spaceship, but he doesn't have enough pieces."

"But if you mix them up, how will you know which ones are yours?" Jane asked, wishing the answer would be that he was giving all of his to Elliot. As much as she'd invested in them, it would be an unbelievable luxury to know she'd never step on one of them in the dark in bare feet again.

"Oh, we'll remember," he said, dashing her hopes.

"Promise me you'll take them away with you when you go to college," she said wanly.

"Yeah, sure," he said, rolling his eyes.

Jane went inside and tried to wake Katie, without any luck. By the time she'd showered and dressed, Katie was still asleep. "Get her, Willard," Jane said.

Willard didn't know many tricks, but he loved this command. It meant he had permission to leap on a bed. He did so now, giving Katie a sloppy lick.

Katie shrieked, thrashed around, and burrowed under the covers. “Mom! Get him off me. That’s disgusting!”

“Katie, it’s eight-fifteen. You have to be at bible school before nine.”

“That’s centuries away!” came the muffled reply.

“Five more minutes. That’s all. C’mon, Willard.”

By the time Jane had run a brush through her hair, contemplated and rejected the idea of a new perm, and slapped on a minimum of makeup, she could hear Katie crashing around, so she went back outside. Shelley called invisibly from some window of her house. “Going to be there a while?”

Jane looked at her watch and called back, “Seventeen minutes.”

Shelley appeared through the garage door a moment later. “Jane, maybe I shouldn’t tell you this, but your youngest child appears to be running away from home. He’s trudging down the street with a suitcase.”

“Gee, I hope he gets a good job and sends money home,” Jane said. “That’s his Lego collection going to Elliot’s house.”

“For good?” Shelley exclaimed.

“Don’t get your hopes up. Elliot’s mother is no fool.”

"Did you talk to Mike about his job?"

"Mike talked to me first," Jane said. She recounted the conversation.

"So it's common knowledge that somebody pushed the rack over on Stonecipher," Shelley said.

"Well, at least that there's something fishy about it. Maybe if he hadn't been so thoroughly disliked, people might just think the police had time on their hands."

Shelley had brought along a thermal mug of coffee and took a long, cautious sip. "You know, somebody must have liked him. Didn't he have adherents to any of his causes?"

"Oh sure, but then he'd move on to another cause and lose them. Nedra Payne practically worshipped him when he was campaigning to outlaw smoking everywhere, including inside people's own houses. She even tried to get me to sign her petition. I wished I'd come to the door with a cigarette so I could have blown smoke in her face. A cigar would have been even better."

"Nedra Payne?" Shelley asked.

Jane blew out her cheeks like balloons.

"Oh, *that* Nedra Payne. The woman with the figure like Kentucky."

"Right. He was her hero until he lost

that one, then he got on the thing about the fastfood restaurants, and she took offense because he made some slighting remark about how she obviously wasn't interested in her health or she wouldn't burden her heart with all that extra weight. And she told *me* all this, expecting sympathy. I just looked at her and said, 'What's your point, Nedra?' "

Shelley laughed. "You're getting better and better, Jane."

"You're my role model. Shelley, what's your take on this? Who would actually kill the man?"

"I haven't got any idea. I know it wasn't me and I'm fairly sure it wasn't you," she added with a grin. "Jane, are you absolutely certain you didn't hear any voices while you were in that bathroom?"

"Oh, a sort of general rumble. There were so many people around. And I could hear somebody talking outside. You remember, people were wandering all over the building and grounds. And I don't often pee with my ear pressed up against the nearest wall. The first unusual thing I heard was the crash of the rack and even that was pretty muffled. I thought somebody had just dropped something heavy. Like a tray of dishes. Except there wasn't that clinking sound dishes would make. Just a couple thumps — I guess that was the hams — and then almost instantly, the big thump."

"If you were right there, why didn't you open the door and see who came out of the room?"

"In the first place, I had no idea it was all that important. Secondly, I had soap all over my hands. I had to rinse them, then took a few seconds looking around for the towel rack. By the time I opened the bathroom door, there were people all over the hallway. All running toward the room. I tried to ooze past, but got caught in the crush and pushed into the storage area. And got myself back out as quickly as I could."

"Who else was in the room then?"

Jane shrugged. "I have no idea. I just saw the rack and the hams all over the floor and Robert Stonecipher in the middle of it. Sort of under the rack. But I could see his head and with that distinctive hair, I didn't even have to wonder who it was. Wait. Sarah Baker must have been in the room and back out before I even got there because somehow she stumbled into me, crying and saying that he was dead. Not he by name, understand. I was horrified that she meant Conrad."

As she spoke, Meow leaped onto the top of the fence that separated the back of her yard from the field behind. There was something that looked like a limp twig in her mouth. "Katie," Jane yelled. "Make sure the kitchen door's closed. Meow has a garter snake."

There was a dramatic shriek and the slam of a door.

"Bloodthirsty things, cats," Shelley said with a shudder. "Speaking of blood — was there a lot?"

"I don't think there was any."

Jane got up and went toward Meow, still perched on the fence. She waved her arms, and the cat jumped back onto the field side. "I used to try to save the snakes," Jane said as she returned to the patio table. "But then I realized that the more snakes Meow kills, the fewer my chances are of ever finding one in my washing machine again."

"I thought I was going to have to get out the sewing machine and whip up a straight-jacket for you the time that happened," Shelley said.

"Shelley, I've got to go in a minute, but the reason I asked who you think killed him is this: when Mel said the guy's wife and business partner were both there and knowing that his secretary was there, too, it made me start thinking. Aren't there all kinds of statistics that murder victims are usually killed by somebody they know really well? And who knows somebody better —"

"— than his wife, partner, and secretary," Shelley filled in. "Still, most people aren't as heartily disliked as he was by so many other people. And while you and I might not think a fight over a zoning problem or the finances of a divorce are motives, it's probably because we haven't been the target of them. Imagine if he was threatening your very livelihood, or your children's future. Think how you'd feel if he'd taken all your money and you couldn't send Mike to college because of it."

Jane nodded. "You could be right. But I, for one, want very badly to know who did this — because of Mike's job." She glanced at her watch and suddenly stood up. "I've got to go."

"Where?"

"To drop Katie off, then help decorate the school for the big graduation party tonight. *Katie — !*"

Several years earlier, after three tragic

graduation night accidents, the high school PTA had decided to accept the fact that the new graduates would stay up and party all night the evening of graduation, and it was better to provide them a place than to let them roam around in vehicles. From a modest beginning, the PTA-sponsored party had assumed gigantic proportions.

There were three bands and dance floors: romantic, country, and hard rock. These were real bands, hired professionals, most of whom were persuaded to work for free or at least reduce their rates for the good cause of keeping the teens alive. There were also "restaurants" set up. The kids could eat and indulge in soft drinks all night long if they had the stomach for it. The decor for the dances and the restaurants was stunning, and the wealthier parents had been known to spend outrageous sums to one-up one another in decorating their assigned areas. There were movie rooms, where videos played endlessly; a fashion show for the girls; and an area where the boys who were a bit behind in their hormonal development and would rather play basketball than mess about with girls could do so.

But the centerpiece of the graduation night festivities was the casino. Real casino equipment, slot machines, roulette wheels, and all the other appurtenances were rented and set up along the main hallways. But instead of actual money, the kids were issued a set amount of fake money with which to play.

During the year the PTA's primary activity was soliciting prizes to be given by drawing or purchased with fake gambling proceeds. A strict and highly complex computerized system had been developed and honed to make sure that every student got one and only one prize, but some of them were doozies. This year there were five televisions, two computer-printer combinations and a laptop, a half dozen airline vouchers, numerous fancy telephones, little dorm room–sized refrigerators. CD players, wireless speakers and headphones, concert tickets, camping gear, exercise equipment, and clothing. In addition, there were hundreds of gift certificates for gasoline, dress shops, office supply stores, restaurants, music stores, and software stores. Students' names were entered only for those prizes they were interested in, so everybody was sure to end up with something he or she wanted.

Jane, as the mother of three kids in the school district, wasn't expected to take a big role in the process for the first child. The PTA philosophy was that if you worked first-timers to death, you'd never get them back. So her assignment was to help with the decorating of the casino/hallways. She'd also have to stay up all night as a door guard to keep the kids from wandering off. That was the part she was dreading, not having actually stayed up all night since the night Todd was born — and not by choice then. The nurses had claimed she was the only maternity patient they'd ever had who thought sleeping through labor was an achievable goal.

When Jane arrived at the school, a few minutes after nine, it appeared to be a madhouse. The building swarmed with parents; a caravan of large trucks was unloading tables, chairs, and sound system gear. The one person who didn't seem to be frantic was Patsy Mallett, the amazing woman who oversaw the whole operation. Jane caught sight of her, sailing serenely through the chaos.

Jane reported to the head of the casino committee and was given a stepladder and a trolley that was stacked high with dark fabric, tacks, a hammer, and a box full of large cardboard-and-glitter stars and moons.

"Start to the south of the main door, overlap the fabric exactly two inches along the ceiling molding, and put two stars and moon on each section," were the curt orders she was given by a woman so overorganized, she made Shelley seem like an aimless slob.

Jane did as she was told, and was just ready to climb down from her ladder and admire her first section of work, when she looked down and recognized the top of Mel's head. He stood just inside the door, notebook in hand.

"Mel, we have to stop meeting this way," she said.

— 6 —

"This is taking the prize for my most tedious investigation," Mel complained two hours later. He'd been roaming around the school, trying to locate and interview a number of the many people who'd been at the deli opening. Not only was it hard to find them, but getting them to stop their work and talk to him was nearly impossible.

But Jane did notice that a number of women took the time to look him over pretty carefully. Too bad he wasn't smiling — that dimple when he smiled would have made them topple off their ladders. At least it always made Jane feel as if she were toppling off something.

"I've heard of nine-day wonders, but this is hardly a nine-hour wonder," he said to Jane, who was taking a short break from her job. "Nobody seems to care that this guy died in their midst."

"It's not that they don't care — well, that's part of it — but they're busy, Mel," Jane explained. "There's so much to be done here and a very short time to do it. Most of these people have been planning this for a year, and now it's show time at last. They're like a great big Olympic team that's been training forever and now they're down to the wire. The woman in charge of this hallway stuff I'm doing had actually practiced and timed putting the stuff up."

"So how come you get to come sit outside? Aren't you wrecking the schedule?" he said grumpily.

Jane ignored his bad temper. He was often this way at the beginning of an investigation. As he started accumulating information, he'd cheer up. "Oh, she built in a break, efficient woman that she is," Jane said with a laugh. "Besides, there was a glitch and I'm missing a box of glittery stars."

"What a weird world you live in," he said.

"Not really. You just haven't done a lot of volunteer work, Mel. It has to be treated like a real job to be effective."

"Well, I'm not being very effective at my real job," he said.

"As far as nobody caring — he not only wasn't very well-liked, but they don't have kids in the school district," Jane said.

"What have kids got to do with it?"

"A lot. Most of the people I know well, for example, are either fairly close neighbors," she said, ticking the categories off on her fingers," or people I do business with, or people I know through the kids and their activities. Not just school stuff specifically, but car pools, sports teams, lessons, recitals, stuff like that. The Stoneciphers were neighbors and some people had business dealings with him, but without kids, they're out of a big part of the loop. Actually, I think they have a daughter, but she's older and must not live at home with them. At least, I've never met her. Of course, his wife was involved in some civic stuff. In fact, she's a born organizer. And he involved himself in lots of things, but his chosen role was always antagonistic to somebody. Or a lot of somebodies. So if people seem to be callous about his death, those are a couple of the reasons."

"It's not just that they're callous," Mel said. "That's okay. A lot of people who get themselves killed aren't terribly well-liked. And I've investigated cases where nobody even knew the victim, they just happened to be witnesses. No, it's that there were such a mob of people at the deli and nobody seems to be able to pinpoint where anybody was at any given time. I can't even begin to get a fix on where anybody was when the rack was pushed over. Like you, a lot of them know where they were at the time they heard the crash, but unless they were actually speaking to someone at the time, they can't say where anybody else was."

"It was a social thing, Mel. Nobody knew they needed to pay any attention."

"I know. I know. But it's making me crazy anyhow. So far all I've got is a milling crowd and nobody who admits to being first on the scene or can tell me who else was. And I'm not even sure it matters."

"What do you mean?"

"Just that there's a second door to that storeroom. Somebody could have pushed over the rack, dodged out the door, come back in another door and acted surprised with the rest of the mob."

"But I thought I heard voices outside. Did anyone see someone come out the door?"

Mel shook his head. "Nope. But the door leads to a covered passage where they store trash containers."

"Oh, right. The trellis thing with the honeysuckle growing on it. I remember seeing that. And there are two doors opening onto it?"

"Right. One from the storeroom and one opening onto the kitchen. You could go out one and in the other without being noticed unless you crashed into the trash and drew attention to yourself."

"Mrs. Jeffry?" a voice called shrilly.

"Oops, I have to get back to work," Jane said, getting up hurriedly. "Mel, you're not going to poop out on chaperoning with me tonight, are you?"

"Nope, I'll probably fall asleep standing up, but I'll be here."

"Shelley, the police aren't getting anywhere," Jane told her an hour later. Jane was folding a pile of table napkins as Shelley finished ironing each one.

"Come on, Jane. He was just grousing to you about his job. And he's not the entire police force. You have no idea what else they know that Mel's got no reason to tell you about."

"Like what?"

"Like fingerprints on the rack for example. Maybe they already know who did it and Mel is just trying to get additional information to enhance their case, not prove anything. Hey, you're supposed to fold them, not wad them up."

"Hmm, I didn't think to ask him about fingerprints. But I can't believe he'd be acting so discouraged if that were the case." She meticulously refolded the napkin and held it up for Shelley's inspection.

"Better. Look, Jane. Suppose for some reason you had to interview everybody at the grade school graduation and find out where everyone was for every minute. Can you think of anything more tedious and boring?"

"Okay, I'd be cranky, too. But according to him, it's a lost cause because of the doors and that little trash barrel area behind there."

"All right. He's got the lousy assignment. So what?"

"So I think it wouldn't hurt if we could give him some useful information. You know perfectly well people will be a lot gabbier with us than with him."

"You know how he feels about you butting in," Shelley said, laying out the last napkin on the ironing board and spritzing it with water.

"What I have in mind isn't butting in. It's just being neighborly. We really should make a sympathy call on Rhonda Stonecipher. We'd do that anyway, even if Mike didn't work at the deli and I wasn't frantic to see this thing solved."

"True," Shelley admitted.

"And we ought to send flowers to Sarah Baker at the hospital, and it would be much nicer if we delivered them in person."

Shelley finished pressing and unplugged the iron. She set it on the kitchen counter and folded up the board. "That's a little iffy. But you're the one who's going to have to explain it to Mel, not me."

"Unless we learn something interesting, there won't be anything to explain," Jane said.

They arrived at the Stonecipher house at the same time as a florist's delivery truck. Tony Belton came to the door, accepted the flowers, and looked at Jane and Shelley as if he'd never seen them before. He was in a suit today and had adopted an appropriately mournful look. With his stunning pale blue eyes, he did it well.

Jane introduced herself and Shelley, reminding him that they had sons on the soccer team he was coaching, and said, "We just wanted to tell Rhonda how sorry we are."

"Come in," he said. "She's just meeting

with the funeral people. I think they're almost finished. Would you like some coffee or a soft drink? Or something to eat? There's a whole houseful of food."

"You go back to Rhonda," Shelley said, looking around. There were flower arrangements shoved everywhere and boxes of food where there weren't flowers. "We could put some of this away for you."

He looked around at the chaos piling up and smiled with gratitude. "That would be great. You sure you don't mind?"

"Not a bit," Jane said. "We'd be glad to be of some use."

Tony disappeared, and Jane and Shelley got busy straightening out the neighbors' offerings. They carried all the food items to the kitchen, and while Shelley rearranged the refrigerator to make room for some casseroles, Jane set the flowers around the living room as artfully as she could. When Jane rejoined her friend in the kitchen, Shelley was shaking her head in wonder. "I'm going to wrap these two hams and put them in the freezer. Why on earth would anybody send hams to the family of a man who died under a pile of them?"

"It wasn't really a pile. And maybe they didn't know. There's probably another freezer in the basement or garage," Jane said quietly. "They've got everything else. This kitchen could give the deli a run for its money. What's that gadget?"

"I think it's a juice extractor."

"One of those things that can turn cabbage into a drink?" Jane asked. "I can't imagine wanting to drink the juice of something that doesn't *have* juice. Like carrots. Give me one of those hams. I'll see if there's a freezer downstairs."

When she returned a few minutes later, she looked stunned. "What a basement!" she exclaimed. "There's a pool table the size of Oregon down there. And the tiles on the floor have silver dollars embedded in them!"

Shelley giggled. "Sounds like the recreation room of a whorehouse."

"Whorehouses have recreation rooms?"

"I don't know, Jane! It just sounds nouveau riche and trashy. The rest of the house is gorgeous though. Did you get a load of the dining room table? I priced those when I was shopping for my new table, and they're damned near as expensive as a car."

Jane lowered her voice to a near whisper. "Wouldn't you think if you had that kind of money, you'd be contented?"

Shelley shrugged. "I guess people tend

to be either happy with life or not. But if I had a house like this, you'd never get me out of it." Although the Stonecipher house was larger than its neighbors, it gave no hint from the outside that it was so elaborate inside. An old house, it had undergone tremendous renovations. The living room, dining room, and kitchen had been large rooms and had been rendered enormous-looking by the removal of most of the supporting walls, which had been replaced with graceful pillars. The floor levels had been changed as well. The living room was a huge sunken area with a pale peach-tinged marble floor showing in small patches between the many fine Oriental rugs. The dining room and kitchen were up two steps. The walls of the entire large area were done with a light-colored grass-cloth that added to the spacious impression. When Tony Belton had gone to rejoin Rhonda, he had passed through large double doors at the far end of the dining room, presumably to rooms beyond the "public" area.

"Wouldn't you love to explore?" Jane said.

"I'll toss you for who gets to take them coffee," Shelley said with a grin.

But this plan was doomed. The funeral

director and his assistant departed before the coffee could brew. Rhonda showed them to the door, then approached the kitchen area. “Jane! Shelley! How wonderful of you to come help me out at this awful, awful time. I burst into tears when Tony told me you were here. I knew I could count on you. Such good friends.”

She folded Jane into an embrace scented with a perfume Jane didn’t recognize, but guessed was terribly expensive. Then, still holding Jane’s hand tightly, Rhonda hugged Shelley. “What would I do without you two,” she said.

Rhonda Stonecipher was, as always, beautifully dressed. Today it was cream linen slacks with a matching blouse and summer-weight sweater. Her hair looked freshly set, her makeup flawless, and she even had on exquisite earrings and a coordinated bracelet. Jane tried to accept this as normal, even though she could vividly remember the day after her own husband had died. Jane recalled standing at the closet door and staring blankly at the contents as if she’d never seen clothing before and had no idea what to do with it. Expertly matching jewelry to a stylish outfit would never have crossed her mind.

But then, it seldom crossed her mind in

normal circumstances either unless Shelley reminded her.

"We're so sorry about your loss," Jane said.

"It was a terrible shock," Rhonda admitted. "But everyone's been so kind. Dear Tony has been helping me with the arrangements for the funeral." With that, she let go of Jane and Shelley and transferred her grip to Tony, who looked a little startled, but pleased. "Tony helped me decide on the coffin. Such a terrible word, coffin. And such a terrible thing to have to decide about. And the funeral people asked me all sorts of things that I never gave a thought to. Like things for the obituary in the paper, for example. Robert's degrees and professional organizations and exact dates. Tony had it all in a file. No wonder Robert was so pleased to have him for a partner."

She was babbling, but she was entitled to, Jane figured. "Sit down and rest," Shelley said. "The coffee's done and you really should eat something. Jane and I will bring it out to you."

Dabbing at the corners of her eyes, careful not to mess up her makeup, Rhonda let Tony lead her away to the sofa grouping in front of the enormous fireplace in the sunken living room. Shelley gave Jane a quick look that silently said, "We already have things to talk about."

When they joined Rhonda, Tony had disappeared again. "He's making some phone calls for me," Rhonda explained without prompting. "The state bar association and some old friends and neighbors. Oh, dear — it doesn't seem possible that this has happened, does it?"

"It's a terrible shame," Shelley said. "And it must be very hard on you."

"Yes, but it could have been much worse for Robert." At their perplexed expressions, she added. "You see, he had an absolute horror of illness and a lingering death. He was so active — so enormously active. Physically, mentally, socially. To have been rendered inactive would have been hell for him. At least his death was very, very quick. I know if he'd had a choice, that would have been his preference."

"Do the police have any idea what happened?" Shelley asked innocently.

'They're not telling me anything," Rhonda said with what would have been called a pout in other circumstances. "Just asking questions. Terribly personal questions, some of them."

Tony Belton had come back into the

room. "— which I keep telling you you're under no obligation to answer," he added.

"But Tony, I have nothing to conceal. And I want the person who did this awful thing apprehended as soon as possible."

Tony didn't comment, but held out the list of names and phone numbers. "Rhonda. I think one of these is wrong. I keep getting a pizza restaurant."

The doorbell rang and Tony started to get up. Shelley stopped him. "I'll get it. In fact, Jane and I need to be moving along. We'll come back later on and help with the food, or tidying up or whatever you might need."

They went to the door, where two more neighbors stood. One had a box of pastries from an expensive bakery. The other had a foil-covered casserole in a raffia basket. Shelley showed them in, and as she was closing the door, they could hear Rhonda saying, "Martha! Nancy! How wonderful of you to come help me out at this awful, awful time. I knew I could count on you. Such good friends."

"Hmm. Why does that sound familiar?" Shelley said.

— 7 —

"Why are we rushing off?" Jane asked.

"Because she's not a real person. She's a recording. She's not going to say anything interesting or useful. Not unless you're willing to be patronized for days on end while you wait."

"But did you see the looks she was giving Tony Belton?"

Shelley nodded. "That's a woman who is either having an affair or wanting to have an affair."

"I agree. There was something hungry and greedy in the looks, the little touches, the sad but provocative smiles. I wonder if Mel has seen them together. Do you think a man would pick up on that?"

"Even if he did, it wouldn't be evidence —"

"But it's sure a nice motive, isn't it?" Jane said, getting into the car. "The wife and partner could get all the benefits of his business, his investments, everything — and without the bother of having him around. Which has to be a relief to both of them on general principle. A person like that can't be easy to live with or do business with."

"Do you really think we ought to go to visit Sarah in the hospital?" Shelley asked.

"Why not?"

Shelley shrugged. "I'd feel perfectly all right about it if she were in for surgery, but a mental breakdown? What do you say to somebody who's gone off the deep end?"

"The same things you say to anyone. Hope you're feeling better. Chat about neighborhood news — well, maybe not. Let's deliver the flowers and ask at the nurses' station if they think she'd like company. She probably doesn't. And if she does, we'll just be cheerful."

They stopped at a florist shop and got a couple sprays of fragrant pink lilies in an especially pretty clear vase. "We're bringing these for Mrs. Baker," Jane said at the nurses' station when they finally found the right floor. "Should we leave them with you, or —"

"Yes, dear. Leave them here. Mrs. Baker is only authorized to have family visitors. You aren't family, are you? Oh, here comes her sister. She might want to take them in for you."

Grace Axton, looking very tired, had just come out of a room down the hallway. "Oh, how lovely of you," she said, when she saw them standing there with their flowers. "I'll just take them to her room. She's sleeping right now. She'll be so pleased."

Jane and Shelley waited patiently for Grace to return. "You look exhausted," Shelley said when Grace rejoined them. "Let us buy you some lunch. I'll bet you didn't get any."

Grace smiled. "I don't think I have eaten, come to think of it. But not here. The food in this place makes me think of that old movie *Soylent Green*. There's a pizza place across the street."

"You'd eat pizza?" Jane said in amazement. "On purpose?"

When they'd walked across the street and were seated on remarkably uncomfortable rigid plastic chairs, Jane asked, "How is your sister doing?"

Grace lifted her shoulders. "Still sedated. The doctor thinks it was just exhaustion, topped off by that awful man dying in the storeroom. He says a couple days of enforced rest ought to put her right."

"Meanwhile you're doing her work and yours," Shelley said.

"The work's not bad. I'm not much of a cook and Conrad found someone to help him from a restaurant that's shut down for renovations. It'll really screw up our budget, but mainly I'm concerned with Sarah."

Jane said, "Is there anything we can do for her? Bring her magazines or newspapers or some kind of craft project to occupy her?"

"I can't think what," Grace said. "Certainly not newspapers. Conrad would flip. He won't even allow that little local rag in the house because he didn't want her to know about the zoning battle."

A perky waitress came and took their orders. When she'd gone, Shelley said hesitantly, picking her words with care, "I'm a little surprised at the change in Sarah. I remember her in high school as very outgoing, bubbly —"

"— and I was the shy, nerdy one," Grace said.

"Not nerdy, but shy — yes. It's like you've changed roles. What happened?"

"With me, it's simple and not very interesting. I married a jerk and finally got up the courage to divorce him. I'd taken all those bookkeeping classes in school and found out that I was pretty good at numbers and could earn my own living. Once I'd done that, it was like a great revelation that I could control my life! Funny how some of us have to be slapped upside the head with something traumatic to understand that, while others —"

"Like Sarah —" Shelley prompted.

Grace nodded. "Of course, Sarah's trauma was so much worse than mine."

"I don't mean to pry," Shelley said, "but I have no idea what you mean by that."

"You don't know? Really?" Grace asked. "I'd have thought the old school grapevine reached everybody."

Shelley shook her head.

"You haven't heard about the baby?"

"I heard they lost a child, but I didn't know if it was a miscarriage or what and I wasn't sure it was true."

The waitress brought their salads and Grace picked at hers. "They had a child with severe brain damage. Extremely severe. Unable to survive without a hideous array of machines. Constant convulsions. It was unbelievably awful. Sarah had been trying to get pregnant for years. Desperately wanted the child, had a devastating delivery that made it impossible for her to have more children. In spite of that, and because she believed the child was suffering horribly, Sarah wanted the life support removed. The hospital agreed. Unofficially, of course. But they couldn't allow it without a court order. Sarah never left the baby's side. The hospital had to put a guard on her to make certain they couldn't be accused of having benignly ignored the possibility that she might turn off the machines. So she never even had any private moments with the baby."

"How awful for her," Jane said, knowing ordinary words couldn't begin to express what it must have been like for the grieving mother.

The waitress arrived with their pizza and the subject was dropped while they divided it up and sampled it. Finally, after eating only one slice, Grace continued. "They had to go to court to get an order to disconnect the machines. But the judge refused to agree. The baby lived another month."

"I'm sorry," Shelley said, handing Grace a packet of tissues from her purse. "I had no business asking about this and upsetting you more."

Grace mopped her eyes and blew her nose. "No, it's okay. I haven't talked about it in years and I need to every once in a while. It sort of builds up inside and needs to be let out. I had to quit my job to go stay with Sarah for that last month. When the baby finally died, I thought it might be the beginning of Sarah's healing, but she went completely to pieces. She was almost catatonic. When she finally came around, she was a completely different person. Shy, withdrawn, nervous, afraid of everything. It was like losing her, too. She wasn't Sarah anymore."

"What a loss for you, too," Jane said. "Is she your only sibling?"

Grace nodded. "And as strange as it seemed to others that the bubbly cheerleader and the bespectacled nerd sister got along, we were always very close until then. Anyhow, she was released from the hospital and she and Conrad took off roaming around. I guess you've heard they cooked for logging camps."

Shelley nodded. "Your grandmother told my mother that."

"All over the west — Oregon and Washington mainly. Like a pair of hippies, except they were kind of late to qualify. I don't think they ever stayed anywhere more than a couple months. As if they were afraid of making friends or forming bonds with anyone."

"— and having them broken, like with the baby?" Jane asked.

"I guess so. Not that Sarah would say so. Sarah wouldn't say anything personal. We became cordial acquaintances. She always let me know how to reach them if I needed to. Our parents had died before this all happened, but our grandmother was still living and Sarah was concerned about her. It was the one thing we still shared, our love of Gramma."

"My mother thought the world of your grandmother," Shelley said, taking back the tissues and dabbing at her own eyes.

"She was a lovely person. I moved in with her and took care of her for the last year, and she was never once pathetic or self-pitying. Better than I can claim."

"But she left the house to both you and Sarah?" Jane asked.

"Oh, yes. I insisted. She wanted to leave it to me, but once I made her understand that I wanted her to leave it to both of us, she went along with that. She and I both thought that if we could just get Sarah back home, she'd be helped by some kind of hometown magic."

"It still might be true," Jane said. "This is a setback, but the doctor could be right that it was mostly the strain of opening the deli that got her down."

"Maybe," Grace said. But she didn't

sound much as if she meant it.

"Had she changed any?" Shelley asked. "Since they've been back here, I mean? I'd think the very fact that she and Conrad were willing to stay here and set up the deli instead of selling the house was a good sign."

Grace considered this. "I think it was mainly Conrad's idea. And she feels that after all he's been through with her, she owes it to him to do what he wants for a while. Of course, that's the silliest sort of speculation. She's never said a word to me about what she wants or thinks or feels."

"Never?"

"Oh, she talks. She tells great stories about their life in the lumber camps. She has a gift for saying a few things about a person and you feel you know all about them. And they came across a lot of real characters. To tell the truth, I found myself really envying the complete freedom of their life. Always a new place, new people, new sights. Jane? You're frowning. You wouldn't agree?"

"Sorry, but no. And you might not either if you'd grown up that way. I never went to the same school for two years in my life. You and Shelley may not have been in constant touch all these years, but you have something in common that I'm green with jealousy about — a common past."

"Oh, Jane," Shelley said, "don't be maudlin. You know I've given you half my past."

Jane laughed. "Only the dirty, wrinkled parts."

"The dirty parts are the best," Shelley said. "Grace, didn't Sarah show any enthusiasm about opening the deli? Was she actually antagonistic about doing it?"

"Oh, no. She's not antagonistic about anything. You give her a job to do and she does it. And does it well, promptly and cheerfully. But in a strange way, that's what makes her so frustrating. You keep waiting for the spark of genuine enthusiasm — about anything — and it never comes. It's as if she's a really competent actress, but not a brilliant one who can make her character come alive."

"Have you tried to get her to a shrink?" Shelley asked bluntly.

Grace didn't take offense. "Of course. But she just looks at me like I'm the one who needs help and says she's perfectly all right and why would I think otherwise. In fact, that's the only dispute — if you could even call it that — I've had with Conrad. I suggested to him that she might benefit from some professional help and he cut me down like a cornstalk. No. That sounds nasty. He was quite pleasant and polite about it, but made it clear it wasn't even to be considered. And I can see his point, in a way."

"Which is?" Jane asked.

"That he's taken good care of her all this time, and just because she doesn't want to spill her guts every time someone asks her a question, that doesn't mean there's anything wrong with her. He says he loved the girl she was and as they've both grown up, he's come to love the dignified, restrained woman she's become. In fact, he made me feel pretty silly about it."

"How's that?"

"Oh, as if I were trying to recapture lost youth or whatever. He asked me why anybody would want to stay what they were at eighteen. And he's right. But I miss the sister I once had just the same."

"Grace, I've got a frantic schedule today and tomorrow," Jane said. "But if there's anything, however trivial, I can do after that, I will."

"Me, too," Shelley said, grabbing the check as Grace reached for it.

"Thanks. I'll let you know. But for now you've done wonders for me, letting me babble this way. And thanks for a"— she paused and looked down at the remains of the pizza with an ironic grin — "for a 'decent' lunch."

"I think 'decent' is stretching it," Shelley said wryly. " 'Barely edible' is more like it."

— 8 —

When Grace had left the restaurant, Shelley said, "Whew! What a terrible thing for Sarah. And for Grace, too. Imagine if your own sister turned into a stranger."

"I can't imagine," Jane said, toying with a breadstick. "But I'd like to. I think I'd pay somebody big bucks to give my sister a personality transplant."

"Jane! You don't mean that."

"Shows how much you know. But it is awful for Grace. Still, I wonder if Conrad isn't right. Maybe Sarah *is* perfectly happy in her own way."

"Jane, she's in a mental ward! They don't put you in those places for no reason."

"I don't mean this minute, but in general. If you'd had something that emotionally wrenching in your past, it would be bound to change your personality. Likely make you more quiet and private."

"But she's shy, and as a former shy person, I can tell you it's not a happy state."

"I'll never believe this story that you were a shy kid."

"I got over it," Shelley said firmly. "All of which is beside the point. We set out to dig up information about Robert Stonecipher's death, and never talked to Grace about it at all."

"I know. As detectives, we're pretty lousy. We haven't learned anything today, except that Rhonda Stonecipher is a fake person with excellent taste, a lot of money, and the hots for her deceased husband's law partner, and she had a good motive for getting rid of him. And that motive — the desire to be a rich widow — was a given anyway. All we've added to the mix is the part about Tony Belton and we aren't going on anything but instinct on that."

"I'm not sure motive is all that important," Shelley said. "Well, it's important of course, but think about it — if you wanted to bump off your husband so you could get your hands on his money and his protege, wouldn't you plan it better? If you were Rhonda, I certainly think you would. She doesn't leave anything to chance."

"Hmm. You've got a point. But why would you choose unfamiliar territory, a really weird 'weapon,' and do it in the midst of a mob of people, any one of whom might walk in on you and catch you?"

"For that matter, why would *anybody* commit a murder that way?" Shelley added.

"Nobody'd plan one that way, so it had to be spontaneous, didn't it? The heat of passion? Hot words, flouncing around, maybe some shoving."

"And anybody might succumb to the passion of a moment."

Jane rummaged in her purse for her car keys. "Almost anybody but Rhonda. I can't imagine she has an ounce of passion in her. She can probably make love and polish her nails at the same time."

They paid their bill and headed back to the hospital parking lot, where they wasted ten minutes searching for the car on the wrong parking level before discovering where they were.

"Jeez! I thought a really demented car thief had taken the old station wagon," Jane said when they found it. "What a pity it wasn't true."

When they were back into traffic, Shelley said, "But what about Tony Belton?"

"What about him?"

"Maybe he's passionate. Hot-tempered."

"Naw, he's too pretty. Those *GQ*-looking guys have ice water for blood."

Shelley turned and stared at her. "What in the world do you know about that?"

"Nothing," Jane admitted cheerfully. "You could be right. We don't know much of anything about him. And with a scheming older woman shoving him along — who knows what he might be goaded into doing. She's a prize schemer."

"So how can we find out more about him?"

Jane pulled into her driveway. "I don't know, but if it involves attending more soccer practices, I'm out. I can hardly sit through the games without going into a coma."

They got out of the car and Shelley picked up the local combination newspaper/shopper that was lying in the grass between their driveways. She opened it first, as always, to the "Vital Statistics" section with the births, deaths, marriages, and divorces. "Is this yours or mine?" she asked.

"Doesn't matter. I don't read it anyway. I used to check the school lunch menus so I could pack lunches on the days they had things the kids despised, but then one memorable day I had a blinding flash of realization that the kids were capable of opening a paper and reading it themselves, not to mention packing a lunch. It was like getting religion."

"Good God! Jack and Chelley O'Brien had another baby. She's our age and Jack's nearly fifty!"

Jane shuddered. "That would be like having your own grandchildren. Nursing bras and Geritol at the same time."

"Pacifiers and walkers."

"Diapers and Depends."

Shelley laughed. "You win."

"And the prize is a nap," Jane said, heading for the kitchen door. "I have to do a big family dinner, attend the graduation, then stay up all night as chaperone at —"

"Oh!" Shelley exclaimed. She rattled the newspaper pages. "Look at this!"

"What? Hold it still!"

"There. Right there. Under 'Divorces Filed.' Rhonda against Robert Stonecipher. Filed the day before yesterday. The day before she was widowed!"

A car was coming up the street and pulled into Jane's driveway. Suzie Williams got out and moved toward them like a warship under full sail, her platinum hair shining in the sunlight. Her face fell when she saw the shopping paper. "No! You've already seen it, haven't you?" she asked, prodding with a long, scarlet fingernail at the newspaper in Shelley's hands. "I thought for once in my life I might get ahead of Gossip Central. Damn!"

Shelley was still staring at the paper. "Filing for divorce the day before he died! Talk about feeling guilty."

"Guilty, hell," Suzie scoffed. "Think of the relief. You aren't the kind of Pollyanna who believes you divorce a bad-tempered lawyer and come out of it with anything but your second-best underwear, do you? Take it from somebody who's been there, done that, and got the T-shirt to prove it. But with him dying, there's no alimony, no nasty little settlements. She just walks with the whole wad."

Jane almost missed her nap. There was no way she could sleep without thrashing out this news. First she called Mel, who said curtly that he already knew about the divorce and would she please mind her own business and stay out of it.

"I think I've blighted my evening," Jane said, hanging up.

"An evening of chaperoning high school graduates is blighted by definition."

"But what does this do to her motive — or Tony Belton's? If she was divorcing her husband anyway, why would she need to kill him?"

"I can think of a lot of good reasons," Shelley said, perusing the inside of Jane's refrigerator. "Starting with the obvious ones Suzie mentioned. Oh, you're doing a turkey breast for dinner. Good idea."

"The whole meal is Mike's favorites. We're having Thanksgiving in June tonight. What are you looking for? The cream's already out."

Shelley sat down, casting a quick, longing look at the coffeemaker, which was burbling along at its own slow pace. "Okay, Rhonda filed for divorce, told her husband, and he said the dreaded words — 'No money.' They argued about it all day and the flames burst out again while they were in the deli. Suddenly it crossed her mind that she'd come out a lot better as a widow than as a divorcee."

Jane considered it. "Yeah, maybe. But could she possibly be naive enough to think he'd just open his checkbook and say, 'Go in peace, my child'? I don't think so. She's not stupid and she knew him well. As smart as she is, she'd probably changed all their bank accounts to her name only before she ever told him about the divorce."

"But there might not have been much free cash to convert to her name," Shelley said. "If all their assets were in stocks or bonds or something, it wouldn't be possible for her to latch on to much of it. And from what we know about Stonecipher, he seems the compulsive type who'd stash his money away pretty carefully in blue-chip investments the minute it came in."

"The thing wrong with this is that it goes back to planning. In the first place, I can't imagine Rhonda letting go of the source of her funds. She had to know that divorcing him was really going to cut into her budget. So she'd be better off financially if he were dead. If we suppose that she's capable of murder, why didn't she make a good plan to start with and kill him off?"

Shelley got up and poured the coffee. "I don't know. Maybe she'd decided that even the money didn't make it worth living with him, but he was even uglier about it than she anticipated."

"How do you mean?" Jane said, blowing on her drink.

"Oh, maybe he'd seen it coming and put everything they owned into a corporation in his name."

"Can you do that?"

"I think if you're a sharp, stingy attorney who thinks his wife is about to make off with your money, there are a lot of things you can do. Remember that doctor who used to live on the other side of Suzie's house? He divorced his wife and went right out, bought a huge house with a pool, drove his fancy cars, lived like a king with his bimbo girlfriend, and she and the kids had to go on welfare."

Jane nodded. "Maybe Stonecipher threatened to dump Tony, too. If he knew about their relationship — if there is a relationship."

"Maybe," Shelley allowed. "But wouldn't a sharp young attorney be able to make it on his own?"

"If he *is* sharp. He may be a lousy attorney — with great legs and to-die-for eyes."

"Then why would Stonecipher take him on?"

"To have someone to do the boring, routine stuff and attract a lot of women clients?" Jane suggested. "But let's assume he was bright. Why couldn't he be the murderer?"

"In cahoots with Rhonda?"

"Let's say not," Jane said. "Suppose Rhonda flings herself at him, says she's divorcing her husband and wants him instead? If he has any sense, he knows he's about to acquire a very expensive woman and will probably end up out of a job besides. Assuming he's interested in acquiring her, what better way to handle it than to get Robert out of the way entirely? He'd get the woman, the business, all the money."

Shelley got up and topped off her coffee. "But we're back to planning versus passion again. This scenario for Tony presumes cold-blooded premeditation, and shoving a rack of hams onto someone in a crowded deli is stupid and dangerous. It seems like a real fluke that anybody got away with it."

Jane sighed. "That's the real problem, isn't it? Why would anybody take a chance like that? It really had to be a spur-of-the-moment thing to do. It's too dumb to be anything else. Or we're too dumb to see the truth."

"Stick your turkey in the oven and take your nap," Shelley said as she got up and rinsed out her coffee cup. "Maybe your subconscious will work out the answer."

"You've got a lot more faith in my subconscious than I do."

"I have no faith whatsoever in your subconscious, but if you try to serve your mother-in-law an undercooked turkey breast, I'll never hear the end of it."

The turkey was a great success. So was

the dressing, the mashed potatoes, the gravy, and the corn casserole. In fact, Thelma Jeffry couldn't find anything to complain about except that cranberry sauce gave her a rash. "Then don't eat any, Grandma," Todd suggested sensibly.

Jane's honorary uncle Jim, a former army officer and lifelong friend of her parents, was there, too, standing in for them. And he was as proud of Mike as a real grandfather. Jane's brother-in-law Ted was there as well, doing his best to be a substitute dad. Ted's wife, Dixie Lee, presented Mike with an envelope containing a surprisingly generous check, and Jane's sister Marty, with her instinctive bad timing, called just as they started eating to wish Mike a great graduation.

"It's too bad your parents couldn't make it here for the big day," Thelma said as they were finishing up what everyone agreed was the best cherry cobbler Jane had ever made.

Mike, recognizing this as the sly criticism it was meant to be, fluffed up like an offended rooster. "Grumps is halfway around the world and they're hosting a diplomatic meeting that's been planned for two years."

"Oh, I didn't mean to imply —"

Jane had to start clearing the table to hide her smile.

"Gotta go, Mom. Everybody," Mike said.

"Mike! You're not wearing Bermuda shorts to graduate, are you?" Jane exclaimed.

"It doesn't make any difference. We're all wearing those silly long black dresses anyway, and the party after graduation is casual."

When Mike had gone, twirling his cap and carrying the hated gown as if it were a lab experiment gone wrong, Thelma said to Katie, "When I graduated from high school, we wore long white gowns and carried roses. It was girls' school —"

While Thelma told her story, which Jane feared would make Katie think going to an exclusive private school might be fun. Jane and Uncle Jim finished clearing the table.

"Sorry your folks aren't here, honey?" he said as he rinsed the dishes and handed them to her to put in the dishwasher.

"Not at all. We've got you," she said, giving him a peck on the cheek.

"You've raised a good boy, Janey."

"I've had a lot of help. And if you say one more nice thing, I'll burst into tears and have to be led, sobbing uncontrollably, to the graduation. I'm having a real sappy week."

— 9 —

The graduation was marvelous. It had all the sentimentality such occasions deserved. The valedictorian gave a talk that relied much too heavily on a thesaurus and was virtually incomprehensible, but had the virtue of relative brevity. The school orchestra, even without the seniors playing, did a more than credible "Pomp and Circumstance." A local minister gave a short inspirational talk that managed to suggest prayer without actually indulging in it. The teacher who read the graduates' names had done her job well, and as far as Jane could tell, didn't mispronounce a single one. She even breezed through the exchange students easily.

The graduates all looked beautiful, even the oily-haired, pimpled ones. It was that kind of event.

Todd was bored senseless; Katie was enthralled; Thelma watched like a hawk for glitches and found precious little to criticize. Mel, who met them at the stadium at the last moment, merely looked glad to sit down. Jane's sister-in-law Dixie Lee, who had no children, but had recently suffered a second miscarriage, cried more than Jane. And Ted, normally an extremely quiet, reserved man, astonished them all, including himself probably, by yelping approval when Mike's name was called out.

The system for keeping all the graduates sober and safe meant they were all funneled directly from the ceremony into the school building. Thelma was indignant until Jane explained that families could go into the school to congratulate their own — if they thought they could find them in the melee. Ted and Dixie Lee offered to wait in the car for her, but were persuaded instead to take Todd and Katie home. Jane's Uncle Jim volunteered to accompany Thelma on her quest and drive her home. Considering that he could hardly stand to be in the same room with her, it was a credit to his devotion to Jane's family and his gentlemanly instincts — or perhaps to his long military training in coping with the enemy and a longing to brush up his skills — that he made this offer.

As they headed toward the building, someone put a hand on Jane's arm. She turned, and it took her a moment to place the woman speaking to her. It was Emma

Weyrich, the aerobics instructor who had also been Robert Stonecipher's paralegal.

"Emma, what are you doing here?" Jane asked. "Do you have a child graduating?"

This was the wrong thing to say. Emma was too young for that and took offense. "Of course not. My sister's daughter graduated tonight. My *older* sister."

"Sorry. Of course. I was just surprised to see you. I'm sorry about your boss."

Emma's normally pretty features hardened. "Yeah, well. It was a surprise."

What an odd reaction, Jane thought. *Not exactly remorseful.*

"Listen, Jane, we need to talk."

"Oh? I can't now."

"I didn't mean here and now. How about tomorrow?"

"Okay, but late in the day."

"What time?"

"Four?" Jane suggested. "Want to meet somewhere?"

"No, come to my apartment," Emma said curtly. She took a little notepad out of her pocket to write an address and handed it to Jane. "Be prompt," she warned Jane, handing her the slip of paper before turning and disappearing into the crowd.

"What was that about?" Mel asked. He'd

gone ahead a ways before realizing he'd lost her.

"I haven't any idea, but it was rude. I've been summoned to her presence. Four o'clock tomorrow and I'm not to dawdle around and be late. She probably noticed the way my skirt fit and wants to harass me into more exercise," Jane said, trying to make light of her anger.

"Don't go," Mel said.

"Why not?"

Mel sighed. "I'll tell you later. When we have some time to talk."

"She's a suspect! You think she killed Stonecipher!"

"Shh. Keep your voice down. No, she didn't kill Stonecipher."

It took Jane only a moment to absorb the implication of this statement. "If you know she didn't, then you must know who did. Has there been an arrest?"

"Jane, keep quiet. Later."

She knew that tone. She stopped asking questions.

Even though she'd worked on the decorations, Jane was astonished when she saw the final transformation of the school. By half-closing her eyes, she could imagine she was in a fancy resort hotel. The materials might be sheets, crepe paper, and dime-store glitter, but the overall look was glitzy and fun. After an hour or so when all the grandmothers, uncles, and little sisters had left, the kids settled in to have a good time.

Someone had thoughtfully provided comfortable chairs at the door Jane and Mel were to guard, and the two of them settled in. They were, unfortunately, just across the hall from the room where the country music band was playing. Jane wasn't much of a fan of country music and decided she'd either be a convert or a raving maniac by the time the night was over. She told herself to remember that it could have been worse. They could have been cheek by jowl with a rap group. Mel slouched and took a nap despite the noise and bustle around them. This performance amazed Jane.

She'd brought along a book to read — one of her many-times-reread Dorothy Sayers mysteries. Comfort books, as she thought of them. None of the kids showed the least interest in trying to go out the door, and she was soon immersed in Lord Peter's adventures.

A little before midnight, the band took an hour break, and the hallway emptied.

The quiet woke Mel up. He roamed away in search of food and eventually came back with chicken salad sandwiches, chips, and soft drinks. They ate in silence, and when they were done, he said, "You're being awfully patient. It's sort of scary."

Jane wiggled her fingers as if barely restraining herself from strangling him. "Mel, I can't stand it anymore. If Emma Whatsername didn't kill Stonecipher, who did?"

"Nobody," Mel said.

"What do you mean? I saw him. He was dead. His wife is getting ready to bury him."

"He died of a heart attack. Natural causes."

Jane sat staring at Mel for a long moment. "But — but if he died of a heart attack, why did somebody make it look like he'd been murdered? Mel, that can't be right! He must have had the heart attack when the rack was pushed over on him. That caused it."

Mel shook his head. "Nope. The coroner was very sure. He had been dead for at least ten minutes, possibly longer, before the rack went over. I got the word just before I left the office for the graduation."

"How — why — ?"

"You sound disappointed. I thought

you'd be pleased to know," Mel said. "You've been in such a froth about Mike working where there'd been a murder. Now he's not."

"Oh, I am pleased. But horribly confused."

"Me, too. But at least it's not a murder investigation anymore."

"No, it's even stranger. Considering how many enemies Robert Stonecipher had, you'd think whoever found him dead would have started organizing a victory parade, not tried to make it look like he'd been killed. Why would anybody make it look like murder?"

"I have no idea. But it's not a homicide investigation anymore and I can file all my notes about who was where and when."

"Why did you tell me not to go to Emma's? Not that I intend to anyway."

"Because I knew you were considering it in order to snoop. And there's no need."

"But surely that's not just the end of it."

"No, I'm sure there's some legal violation in the matter of pushing the rack over on a body. Malicious mischief or something. But it's not my case anymore. I need to stretch my legs for a bit. Do you mind if I go take a look at the setup here? Then I'll spell you if you want to take a nap."

Jane, deep in confused thought, waved him away. "Sure. Go ahead."

She was still brooding on this bizarre twist when Patsy Mallett, the head of the party organizers, came by on her rounds. "How's it going?" Patsy said, taking the chair Mel had vacated and briefly setting down a notebook — her party bible, she called it — on the floor.

Patsy was a large, gap-toothed, dynamic woman in her fifties. Nearly eight years ago, she had first come up with the idea of the school-sponsored all-night party. From humble, non-mandatory beginnings (Jane had heard that the first year only twenty rather nerdy kids had been desperate enough for a social activity on graduation night to attend), the party had become THE thing to do and it was all due to Patsy's tremendous energy and planning. She had the rare gift of being able to juggle fifteen committees without ever seeming flurried or harassed. She greeted every crisis with a smile and a shrug and the comment "Not to worry. It'll work out." And it always did with her at the helm.

"Nobody's tried to make a break for freedom," Jane assured her with a smile.

"No, they don't much anymore. But we promise the parents the kids can't leave unless a parent fetches them, so we have to guard every door. You have two more children coming up through the grades, don't you, Jane?" Jane nodded reluctantly. She knew where this was going.

"And one's a sophomore next year, right?" Patsy went on. "If you'd choose a committee you'd like to serve on next year, then the year after you might co-chair it. Or at least be ready to co-chair when your third one comes along."

"Do you know my friend Shelley Nowack?"

Patsy's eyes lit up. "I've heard of her. I don't believe we've ever met though. I hear she's a very efficient person."

"She is. She's the kind of chairman you need. I'll talk to her about what committee she'd like and serve with her."

"Great. We'll get together next week."

"So soon?"

"Jane, this doesn't happen overnight. Next year's committee chairs are already working. Contracts with some suppliers have to be signed years in advance."

"I'm in awe of how you manage this," Jane said. "Shelley will love knowing you."

"I'll share my secret with her," Patsy said, grinning.

"Secret?"

"Yes. You know each committee has two cochairs. I tell people that's in case one gets sick or has to move. But the fact is, I was a history major in college, and I've always remembered something I learned about Henry VIII."

"Henry VIII?" Jane said, believing she'd misheard.

"Yes. People think he was a womanizing bumbler. But he wasn't a bumbler. He was a very effective monarch, and he managed it by pairing enemies," Patsy explained. "See, kings had to send off ambassadors to all the other European powers, and while the ambassadors were out of the king's sight, he didn't know what they were up to. Sometimes they weren't as competent or as loyal as they could be and went off on their own agenda instead of the monarch's. So Henry always sent two ambassadors together and made sure they didn't like each other. That way they were forever tattling on each other and he knew exactly what both of them were up to. And since each knew the other was tattling, each did the best job he could to show off and impress him. Henry got efficiency and comprehensive reports."

Jane laughed. "You're not nearly as sweet as you look! Shelley is going to love knowing you, Patsy. I can't believe you model yourself on Henry VIII."

"I'm getting his figure, that's for sure, and if I didn't keep up on my estrogen, I'd probably have his beard by now," Patsy said. "Still, it's worked out pretty well as a committee philosophy. And if you ever tell anyone but Mrs. Nowack that I said this, I'll deny ever speaking to you," she added with a smile.

"This is your last child graduating this year, isn't it?" Jane asked.

Patsy nodded. "Last of five. I'm going to start backing off and spend more time on my own business, which is coming along nicely."

"You do all this and have a business, too?"

"Yes, with four of the kids gone, I was driving my husband crazy trying to reorganize him," she said with a laugh. "So I started a billing company. Saves small businesses the cost of a full-time employee for what is really a half-a-day-a-week job. I haven't gotten into medical offices because that's too complex, what with Medicare and insurance, but I have a florist, an office supply store, a secretarial service, and an attorney. Well, I had an attorney until yesterday, but he died."

"Was that Robert Stonecipher?"

"Yes, it was. Did you know him?"

"No, but my son works at the deli where he died and I was there."

"Terrible thing to have happen," Patsy said. "I hear he was killed."

Mel hadn't told Jane the information about Stonecipher having died of natural causes was a secret, but she still didn't feel it was up to her to blab.

So she kept quiet and Patsy went on. "I can't say I'm too shocked, though. I think the man's life was in terrible disarray."

"What do you mean, disarray?"

"With all due respect to the dead, Robert Stonecipher was a nut case. So discontented and angry at everything. None of us can remake the world to suit ourselves and that's what he seemed to be trying to do. All those 'causes' of his! And he always took the line that it was for somebody else's own good. I think most people are like me — they want to make their own decisions about what's to their own benefit, not have some priggish holier-than-thou jerk tell them. He tried it on me. Once! Tried to slither into a discussion about how much healthier I'd be if I lost weight."

"No!"

Patsy smiled. "Oh, by the time I got through with him, he knew better than to ever mention it again. I have children to provide me with gratuitous personal critiques. I don't need them from others."

Patsy and Shelley are going to be soul mates, Jane thought.

"And his personal relationships were just as bad, it seems," Patsy went on. "You know, I presume, that his wife had filed for divorce."

"I saw the notice in the paper."

Patsy was quiet for a minute, then said, "You know, I've been wondering about something — it's pure gossip, which I don't approve of unless I'm the recipient, but since you're dating that detective, I wonder . . ."

This hesitancy was unlike her. "What's this about, Patsy?"

"I'm only telling you this so you can pass it on to your friend the detective, you understand. I went in Stonecipher's office Thursday afternoon to pick up some checks, and he and Emma Weyrich were having a terrific row. I guess they didn't hear me come in and nobody else was around."

"What was the row about?"

"Them. I came into the middle of it and left as fast as I could, but it was about his divorce. I had the impression from what I overheard that he and Emma had been having an affair and she thought now that he was going to be free, she'd be the next Mrs. Stonecipher. He brushed her off."

"I'd heard he had a girlfriend," Jane said. "It never crossed my mind that it was Emma. But it should have. So she was taking the news badly?"

"Very, very badly. Apparently he'd strung her along for years and years. It was really ugly, Jane. I don't like to run off and be a tattler myself, but I wonder if the police ought to know — ?"

"I'll pass this along to Mel, but I don't think you need to worry."

"Good. I didn't want to be one of those old biddies who look like they're out to get somebody. I've never liked Emma, but I don't want to go around sounding like I think she killed him. She was mad, but not that mad. At least, I don't think so."

"Patsy, you were right to pass this along and I'll tell Mel about it, but I think I can assure you that it won't matter."

Patsy gathered up the party bible and rose. "Thanks, Jane. I'll give you a call Monday about getting together with you and Mrs. Nowack and getting the two of you on a committee."

"Why aren't I surprised that you didn't forget that?" Jane asked.

As she watched Patsy leave, she smiled to herself. She thought she'd so cleverly guided Patsy into talking about Robert Stonecipher when, in fact, Patsy had been pulling her along on a leash. Yes, Patsy and Shelley were going to get along well.

— 10 —

"Shelley, I've got to run some errands. Ride along? I have very interesting things to tell you."

"I'm amazed. It's only ten in the morning and you were up all night and you're still able to speak English fairly fluently?"

"I found a cot in the nurse's room at school and got a lovely three-hour nap, then came home at six in the morning and slept till nine. I'm actually pretty close to human today. If you don't count my hair," Jane replied.

"Jane, I never consider your hair. Give me five minutes to gather up some dry cleaning I need to drop off."

A few minutes later, Shelley, nearly buried in a pile of Paul's shirts and suits, was sitting in the passenger seat as Jane backed out of the driveway, carefully avoiding the pothole the family was affectionately starting to call the Grand Canyon.

"I have a ton of interesting stuff to tell

you," Jane said. "But the most interesting is that Robert Stonecipher died of a heart attack a good five or ten minutes, at least, before somebody pushed that rack of hams over on him."

Shelley whipped her head around and looked at Jane as if she were crazy. "What? You mean this?"

"The coroner or pathologist or whoever swears to it. Mel told me last night. He'd just found out. Stonecipher wasn't murdered."

"But somebody made it look like he had been!" Shelley said. "I'm dumbfounded. Why would anybody do that?"

"I've been brooding on it for a while and I can think of two reasons," Jane said. "One sort of reasonable, one sort of goofy. If he had life insurance like my husband did, it would pay double if he died by accident. Double jeopardy — I mean, double indemnity. I always mix those up."

"Pointing to Rhonda," Shelley said.

Jane shrugged. "If he had life insurance with that provision and if she were the beneficiary. But he might have other policies as well. You can have more than one life insurance policy, can't you, if you're willing to pay the premiums?"

"I don't know. I would guess you could.

So he might have had one for the girlfriend you heard about. Or even one that paid to his business."

"Oh, that's something else I learned. The girlfriend is Emma Weyrich and I have lots more about her. What I wonder is, can you insure somebody else's life with yourself as beneficiary?"

"I'm pretty sure you can," Shelley said. "But I don't really know a lot about insurance."

"Then you probably won't know what else I was wondering about which is, if you can insure someone else, can you do it without their knowledge? But this is all wandering from the main point, which is that an accidental death might pay off a lot better than a heart attack."

"Emma Weyrich," Shelley mused. "We should have guessed. She's not the young bimbo I had imagined, but —"

"More of an early middle-aged bimbo," Jane agreed. "But a health nut like he was, and an employee constantly in his company."

Jane pulled into the parking lot of the dry cleaners. It was the Dohertys' new establishment, the one Stonecipher had been trying to shut down. Jane always patronized them because they were a nice couple who deserved all the business they could get. She was curious to know if they'd heard yet about the real cause of Stone-ciher's death, but a teenage girl who was their Saturday helper was at the front counter.

When they were back in the car, Shelley said, "So what's the goofy reason for making a natural death look unnatural?"

Jane eased into traffic and headed toward the library. "To make Conrad look bad. To try to hurt his business by linking him to Stonecipher's death."

"But there's no reason to think Conrad did it just because it happened at the deli."

"I know. But if somebody like that Foster Hanlon person found Stonecipher dead and was still steamed about losing the battle with Conrad and what he imagines is the lowering of property values, he might figure that making the deli look like a dangerous place might hurt Conrad's business enough to shut him down. It doesn't make sense, but it could be the way a nasty old thing like Hanlon would think on the spur of the moment. I admit it's pretty thin, but the fact is I was frantic about Mike working there when I thought it was a murder. Other people might avoid going there for the same reason."

Shelley nodded. "It's possible. Or maybe Conrad had some other enemy who'd like to see him fail. For that matter, maybe Sarah or even Grace was the target, so to speak. I can't imagine disliking either of them. The old Sarah was very well-liked and the new version of her is as bland as a mouse. But I didn't know her well when we were young and don't know her now either. The same goes for Grace. I like her, but really don't know much about her. She mentioned a nasty divorce. Her former husband could be a real vindictive sort."

"But since it's not murder anymore, I don't suppose we'll ever know," Jane said.

She got out of the driver's seat, opened the back door, and gathered up her library books from the floor of the station wagon. "You need anything here? Are you coming in?"

"No, I'm going to sit here and think. You know, Jane, instead of losing interest in this now that it's not a murder case, I find my curiosity piqued. Why risk being hauled in for an imaginary murder? I can't fathom it."

"Me neither. If the autopsy guy hadn't been up to par and it went on the record as a murder, somebody would have been in a lot of trouble. They'd have probably been convicted of a murder they really didn't commit. It was a huge risk. I'll only be a minute. One of these is overdue and I have to pay the fine."

When Jane came back out of the library, Shelley was standing by a trash barrel, the now-empty car ashtray in her hand. She was staring into space.

"You just can't resist cleaning up things, can you," Jane said, jiggling her elbow.

Shelley got back into the car and fitted the ashtray into place. "What if making his death look like murder was meant to get someone else in trouble?"

"Like how?"

"I'm not sure. The idea's still coming together." She thought for a minute. "Okay. How's this? If I really disliked somebody at the deli opening and in innocently wandering around, looking the place over, suppose I came across a dead Stonecipher. I might think, ah-hah! My great enemy Suzie Q is out there wearing that sweater that sheds all over the place. If I push this rack over and make it look like Stonecipher was killed and then shove some of that sweater fuzz under the rack, maybe the police will think she killed him and she'll be in a lot of trouble."

"How would you know how the dead

Stonecipher had died? Or even that he was dead, and not just in a faint? And why would you risk being seen coming out of the storage room not only once, but twice?" Jane asked. And then she laughed. "Not to mention having to go pluck Suzie Q's sweater in full view of a crowd of people."

Shelley didn't look chastened. "Hmm. Guess that one won't fly. Where are we going next?"

"Shoe repair."

"Not the taupe heels again. Jane, why don't you break down and buy new shoes to replace them?"

"Because I love those shoes. If I could get exact duplicates, I would. You know that commercial where the women are playing basketball in their high heels? I could do that in these shoes. If I ever had the desire to play basketball. Which I haven't."

"I did that once," Shelley said.

"Played basketball?"

"No. Got smart when I realized I loved a green plaid blouse better than I'd ever loved a piece of clothing. I went back to the store and they still had one in the same size. I bought it, put it away in the cedar chest, and wore the first one for a couple years until it was almost in tatters. I finally threw it away, feeling terribly smug that I had a replacement. But when I got out the next one, I discovered that it had aged just as fast as the one I'd worn. I wore it twice and it fell apart in the wash. I was crushed."

When Jane had once again entrusted her beloved shoes to the repairman, they headed for the giant discount store where Jane intended to buy a lampshade to replace the one the cats had clawed. But the Saturday parking lot was so full they gave up. "Did you see those perfectly healthy, agile yuppies park in the handicapped place and bound out of their car?" Jane fumed.

Shelley grinned. "My mother gets so mad about that. She had some little cards printed up that she puts under the windshield wipers of people like that. The card says: 'The handicap is mental, I assume.' "

"We *must* have some of those made up!" Jane exclaimed. "If we can't shop, we'll have to eat, I guess."

"Sad but true. Where?"

"The new deli would be great, but we couldn't talk freely there. How about that little salad shop next to the mall?"

When they were seated at a table at the back of the salad shop, Jane said, "I have a real treat for you. A gift from the gods. You know who Patsy Mallett is?"

"Of course. The amazing woman who runs the graduation party."

"Yes, the gift is from her. But I'm afraid there's a bit of a price."

"What kind of a gift comes with a price?" Shelley said, studying the menu.

"Most gifts, I've found," Jane commented. "Anyway, here it is —" She told Shelley the Henry-VIII-and-his-paired-ambassadors theory of committee management.

Shelley was so stunned that she just looked blankly at the waitress when she arrived at the tail end of the explanation.

"What'll you have?" the young woman said.

"I — I don't know. Anything," Shelley said.

"She'll have the chicken Caesar, extra Parmesan," Jane said, "and I'll have the taco salad, no guacamole."

"Jane, this is wonderful! A real forehead slapper. So that's how she accomplishes so much and keeps tabs on everything. Wow! I can't wait to try this out. I need to sit at this woman's feet —"

"That's the payoff part. You're going to. I volunteered us to work on next year's graduation. You choose the committee.

She's calling me Monday to set up a time for us to meet her and talk about it."

"It'll be worth it. How'd she happen to tell you this?"

"She wanted me to pass something along to Mel. About Emma Weyrich. But I'm getting ahead of myself. Quit rubbing your hands together that way about the Domineering Woman's Guide to Bossing People Around and listen to me."

"Okay, okay. I'm with you."

"When the graduation ceremony was over, Emma Weyrich made a point of grabbing me and saying she wanted to talk to me."

"What about?"

"She wouldn't say. All very hush-hush. I said I was sorry about her boss dying and she just brushed it off, which I thought was strange then. Anyway, I didn't know then — and I'm certain she didn't either — that Stonecipher had died of a heart attack. I thought later that she might have wanted to talk about someone she suspected of killing him. Either that, or she was trying to beat us into shaping up again. She was real rude and abrupt and told me to come to her apartment at four o'clock today, just like it was a dental appointment or something."

"You're going?"

"I don't think so, but I am curious. Especially after hearing what Patsy Mallett had to say."

"Which was?"

Jane started to explain about Patsy overhearing the fight between Emma and Stonecipher and broke off when the waitress arrived with their salads. When they were alone again a moment later, she continued, "Patsy suspected Emma, but didn't want to be a gossip," she said. "Of course Patsy didn't know either about the heart attack and I didn't say anything."

"Do you think Emma wanted to confide about this affair in your shell-pink ear?"

"I wondered. But it seems so unlikely. I don't even know her except for having taken that one class. We have virtually nothing in common, so why does she want to talk to me at all? And why was it all so abrupt and almost businesslike? It wasn't a case of her appealing to me for 'let's talk sometime, I need some advice.' It was very much an appointment. A summons, really."

"That is weird," Shelley said, critically examining a piece of the chicken in her salad. "But maybe it's just her manner. I don't recall her being notable for her social grace. And according to Patsy Mallett, Emma had good reason to be pretty badly disconcerted. You know, I think she turned up in town about the same time the Stonecipherss did. She might have come along because he was moving here. Who knows how long this affair has been going on? To have her hopes of marrying him blow up in her face just when she thought she'd finally gotten what she wanted — and then to have him die the very next day — well, it would be a rare person who didn't get badly rattled."

"True, but it still doesn't explain why she'd want to talk to me, of all people, about it. Surely she has friends of her own. I'm barely even an acquaintance. You'd think she'd even know Patsy better. She sees her every week. And if I needed advice, I'd choose Patsy over me any day."

"I think we should find out what it was all about," Shelley said.

Jane broke off a chunk of the taco shell her salad came in and grinned. "Good. I like that 'we' part. You'll go with me?"

"Sure. I'm as curious as you are. Maybe she'll tell us something interesting."

But when they got to Emma's apartment, they discovered that she wasn't telling anybody anything.

She was dead.

— 11 —

The apartment complex was a large, modern one, laid out and landscaped with lots of trees and berms and winding streets in an elaborate way that made it look more cozy and private than it actually was. When Jane and Shelley noticed the ambulance and police car, they assumed at first that there had probably been an accident at the pool. But as they approached the building Emma lived in and saw two suited men who were obviously official at the door of the building, they cast quick, alarmed looks at each other.

They were stopped at the door of Building Three.

"What's happened?" Jane asked.

"Are you residents?" the taller man asked.

"No, we're visiting someone who lives in this building," Shelley replied. "Emma Weyrich in 308D."

"Would you wait here, please," the plainclothes officer said firmly. He gave the other man a quick glance that clearly meant *Make sure they do.*

"Is Mel VanDyne here someplace?" Jane asked. When nobody replied, she added, "Tell him Jane is here waiting to talk to him."

Mel appeared a minute or two later. "Funny, I'm not surprised to see you here," he said, half disgusted, more than half angry.

"Is it Emma?" Jane asked.

He nodded.

"Dead?"

"Very," he said. "A neighbor called half an hour ago. Said he found her cat out in the hallway. Took it home and found the door ajar. Went in and found her."

"How was it done?" Shelley asked quietly.

"A smack in the head with a small barbell-type thing. Prints wiped clean. Very tidy. No struggle. No blood. You'll have to explain yourselves, but not to me." He addressed the officer who'd fetched him. "Smith, will you take statements from these ladies? Mrs. Jeffry and Mrs. Nowack. And don't let *them* interview *you*."

He went back into the apartment building, and Shelley and Jane gave their statement. Jane explained that Emma, whom she knew only slightly, had approached her, setting up an appointment to meet at this address at four. She turned over the slip of paper on which Emma had written her address.

"If you didn't know her, why did you come?" the officer asked.

"Plain old curiosity," Jane admitted.

"And you, ma'am," he said, looking at Shelley. "Were you invited, too?"

"No, I just came with my friend Jane."

"What was this appointment about?" he asked.

"I have no idea," Jane said. "As I told you, I hardly knew her. But her boss died at the deli where my son works. I was present at the time. Maybe she wanted to ask me about it. Or just have someone sympathize. I don't know."

"Sympathize?"

"It was a small office. She might have been out of a job for all I know," Jane said. She'd promised Patsy she'd tell Mel about the argument Patsy had overheard, but she felt she should tell Mel directly. "If you're through with us, I need to get home," she added.

"I guess VanDyne knows where to find you?" the officer asked.

Jane didn't like his wink-wink-nudge-nudge tone, but decided she wasn't in a strong position to get huffy. "I think so," she said stiffly. She and Shelley went back to the car in silence and Jane drove out of the apartment complex and straight through the drive-up lane of a fast-food restaurant on the next corner. She ordered two coffees and pulled over under a shade tree a block away.

"Jeez!" Shelley said. It was the first time she'd spoken since they left Emma's.

They sat sipping their drinks in silence for a long while. "I guess the investigation into Stonecipher's death is back on," Jane said. "Mel's going to find a way to blame me."

"Jane, just think . . . if we'd come early, we might have found her! If you think you're in trouble with him now, imagine what that would have been like."

"Oh, God! You're right, Shelley! We might have even stumbled into the middle of it happening."

The enormity of this rendered them both silent again. Finally, Jane said, "I have to go home and start dinner."

When they reached Jane's driveway, Shelley said, "Call me if you hear anything more from Mel. I just can't take this in."

"I guess the only good thing about this is that it's clearly something personal with Stonecipher's office or home life. Nothing to do with the deli. Thank heaven! Still, I wish Mike had a nice summer job in Timbuktu and none of this had ever happened."

"Where's Mike?" she asked Katie, who was standing in front of the open refrigerator door looking as if she'd come to the end of a long quest and had found out that the prince really was a frog.

"At work. And Todd's upstairs on the phone with Elliot. What's for dinner? There's nothing in here."

Jane joined her. "Somebody ate the last of the turkey, didn't they? I guess I'm going to have to do a grocery store run. Help me make a list."

They sat down at the kitchen table and wrote down everything they'd need for the next couple days. Somehow this included a lot of soft drinks, chips, dip, and even blusher and pantyhose for Katie. Jane looked at the list, put her head in her hands. "I can't face it. I hate the grocery store. I've spent half my adult life there."

"Then let's have something from the deli," Katie suggested. "I want that deviled ham sandwich they make."

"Sounds good to me. Find out what Todd wants. We'll do this grocery run tomorrow."

Jane parked in front of the deli, surprised there weren't more cars around and disappointed that Mike's new truck wasn't among them. Conrad was at the counter. The only other customer was leaving. "I guess Mike isn't around?" Jane asked.

"No, he's making deliveries," Conrad said. "You need him? I could give you the list of addresses and you could try to catch up with him."

"No, I was just wondering. Actually, I need dinner for my family. You've ruined me for cooking."

Grace Axton came in from the kitchen behind the counter area. "Hi, Jane. I thought that was your voice. What do you need?" Jane told her and Grace said, "Conrad, sit down and rest. I can fix these things without messing anything up."

Conrad came around the counter and sat down at one of the little tables with Jane. He was limping. "You've hurt yourself?" Jane asked.

"Just a blister on my heel. Do you mind if I take my shoe off?"

"Not in the least. I hardly ever wear shoes unless I leave the house. And then I can never find a pair that matches."

Conrad took off his shoe, dropped it on the floor, and happily massaged his aching stockinged foot. “That boy of yours is really something, Mrs. Jeffry.”

“Please, I’m Jane. Mike is terrific, isn’t he?”

“Do you realize he came in early and tidied up the yard and mowed the lawn this morning? Nobody asked him to, he just thought it needed doing. What a kid!”

“And he’d been up all night at the graduation party,” Jane bragged. “He’s okay.”

“I think I’m going to need another driver. I thought most people would come in for things, but the delivery service is, so far, much more popular. There’s too much for just him. Grace had to help with the afternoon deliveries. Mike suggested his friend Scott. I guess if Mike says he’s responsible, he really is.”

Jane laughed. “Scott looks like a misplaced beach burn, but he *is* responsible. And the girls adore him. He’ll make your delivery service even more popular.”

“How you doing, Grace?” Conrad called.

“I’m hurrying,” she replied. There was a thud and a muffled “Dammit.”

“Don’t hurry, Grace,” Jane said. “I’m not in a rush. If Conrad would give me a glass of iced tea, I wouldn’t care if it took an hour.”

Conrad limped off to get them both a glass of tea.

"How's Sarah doing?" Jane said when he returned to the table.

"Oh, fine. Just fine," he said too heartily. "Doctor says she can come home tomorrow. She's just overworked. I'll make sure she takes it easier from now on."

Jane waited for him to elaborate, but he said nothing more. "So the business is doing okay? The incident at the opening didn't matter?"

"Incident? Oh, yeah. Made no difference at all. I thought at first that's why so many people were ordering out — because they were afraid to come in — but now I think it's just that they like having their food delivered. Every order has a menu in it, so it's easy to know what we've got without having to see it. In fact, one of the orders Mike's delivering now is for a party. The folks just said to send them a nice casual dinner for six. Didn't even care what it was."

"That's a real credit to you," Jane said.

"I hope so. Hope it keeps on. We thought business would be slower to pick up."

The door opened and Patsy Mallett came in. Conrad hopped up to run behind the counter and take her order. "Jane, you caught me being a lazy slob," Patsy said, joining her at the little table.

"And you caught me, too," Jane said.

Patsy glanced down and rolled Conrad's shoe over with her toe. "What's this?"

"Conrad's got a blister." Jane lowered her voice to a near whisper. "I'll wait for your order to be ready. I need to talk to you."

"I thought you might," Patsy said, speaking very quietly, too. "I was just at the school making sure everything was taken down and properly stored. I heard about Emma from somebody who lives near her."

They waited, chatting about the school party. "Did your son enjoy the party?" Patsy asked.

"He loved it. And he came home with a portable CD player for his truck, which thrilled him," Jane said.

When their orders were both ready, Jane followed Patsy to her car, a station wagon even more beat-up and rust-ridden than Jane's. "Did you talk to your detective friend yet?" Patsy asked.

"I haven't had a chance. I didn't tell him right away because — I suppose you've heard by now — Stonecipher wasn't killed by that rack falling on him. He died of a heart attack."

"I heard that at the school, too, but wasn't sure it was true. But Emma — ?"

"Emma was murdered," Jane said. "She'd

asked me to come over and Mel knows that, so I'm sure I'll hear from him as soon as he's free."

"This puts a different spin on Stonecipher's death, doesn't it?" Patsy said, frowning.

"I'm sure it must. The two deaths must be connected somehow."

"I didn't want to be a busybody and gossip about Emma, as you know. But with her dead, I'll be happy to tell the police anything that might help them. I didn't like her, but I didn't want her killed. And whoever did it has to be stopped."

"Patsy, who else was around when you heard the fight between her and Stonecipher?"

"Nobody that I know of. It was late in the day and there were no clients waiting to see anyone. In fact, the waiting room was empty. I don't know if the receptionist had already gone home or was just in the copying machine room."

"Could she have overheard from there?"

"Probably."

"And was Tony Belton around?"

Patsy thought for a minute. "I didn't see him. And his office door was closed. He'd probably already left, but I wouldn't swear to it."

"Could he have heard them if he were still there?"

"I imagine so. His office and Robert's share a wall. Why?"

"I don't know. I'm just wondering who else might have heard the dispute. Someone else who had an interest. Who is the receptionist?"

"A little mousy girl named Sandy. She looks about twelve, but she's got three kids, so she must not be."

"Might she have been interested in Stonecipher? I mean romantically interested?"

"Oh, no. I think she thought of him as a well-preserved grandpa type. You know how young women sometimes are with older men — talk to them sort of loud like they might be getting deaf. And even though the office was very first-name basis, she always called him Mr. Stonecipher."

"What about Tony Belton? Somebody mentioned that it was unusual for somebody without kids of their own to be coaching a soccer team, but is he married?"

"I presume he was and he does have kids. At least one. There's a picture of a cute little boy on his desk. I asked about it, and he said it was his son who lived with his mother in Seattle or Portland or someplace in the Northwest."

" 'His,' meaning the boy's mother, or 'his,' meaning Tony's mother?"

"The boy's mother. Why?"

"I don't know. Just wondered. Say, Patsy, have you ever been at the office when Rhonda was there?"

Patsy gave Jane a sharp look and said warily, "As a matter of fact, I have. Why do you ask?"

"Well, it's just that when Shelley and I went over to her house yesterday, Tony Belton was there and they seemed . . ." Jane paused, trying to think of a tactful phrase.

Patsy supplied it. "Chummy?"

"To say the least."

"I thought so, too, the one time I saw them together. But I thought maybe it was just her manner with men. Some women get around anybody male and turn into flirts," Patsy said.

"I don't think she's one of them."

"I've got to get this food home before my husband comes looking for me," Patsy said, opening her car door.

"I'm sorry to have been so nosy," Jane said.

"No, the police are surely going to ask me the same things and I might as well start getting my memory in gear."

Jane drove home so deep in thought that she almost missed her own driveway.

— 12 —

Jane had a message to call Mel when she got home. She did so and told him briefly that he needed to speak to Patsy Mallet and why. She gave him Patsy's phone number, and hearing the rush and irritation in his voice, hung up as quickly as possible.

Mike came home, showered, changed clothes, and went back out for the evening with Scott and a couple of his other pals. Katie asked to have her friend Jenny spend the night. Jenny arrived with enough luggage for a European Grand Tour, and the girls disappeared into Katie's room for the evening. Elliot and Todd took over the living room television to watch ninja movies.

Jane tidied up the kitchen and gave Willard a long pet. "Nobody's paid much attention to you lately, have they, old boy?" she said, scratching behind his ears, which he loved. Knowing, by feline radar, that there was affection being given to pets, Max and Meow appeared, wanting their fair share. Jane petted them, and in an excess of fondness, gave them each some vile kitty treats the kids had forced her to buy. The cats loved them, but would probably throw them up somewhere later. They usually did.

Jane had heard that pets lowered your blood pressure, reduced stress, and all sorts of other good things. Most of the time she didn't believe it. Willard, Max, and Meow were normally just three more children to keep tabs on, but this evening, she did find that a visit with them was pleasant and relaxing.

"At least I don't have to put you guys through college or worry that you'll marry somebody who hates me and wants to take you away to Paris to live," she said.

Willard rolled over for a tummy rub and Meow made a gagging noise.

Jane puttered. She started some laundry, changed the kitty litter, threw out nearly everything in the refrigerator, and sorted through some seed packets she'd ordered in January from a catalog and never got around to planting. She considered spending a few hours with Priscilla on the computer, but decided she'd had enough of words and of talking for one day. She wasn't so much tired as she was tired of conversation and of thinking. She needed something mindless. Like cooking. No, nothing in the house to cook. So she cleaned off the kitchen table and got out a jigsaw puzzle.

By nine-thirty, she had the border finished and had almost completed the big building in the middle. The phone rang.

"Got plans for tomorrow morning?" Mel asked.

"How early?" she asked warily.

"Ten?"

"That's possible. I never make the kids get up for church on the first Sunday of the summer. But the pantry is bare. Don't expect breakfast."

"I'll take you out then. We've never had breakfast together. Well, except that one time —" he said with a very pleasant leer in his voice.

Jane blushed. The breakfast he referred to was a room service meal the morning of the first night they'd spent together. And halfway through it, they'd found something much more fun to do than eating. Best meal she'd ever *not* eaten.

"I'm not sure a public restaurant would be suitable for the way we conduct ourselves at breakfast."

"Oh, I think I can manage to keep my clothes on if you can," he said.

She laughed a bit breathlessly and then said, more seriously, “You sound tired. Get some sleep. I’ll see you tomorrow.”

“Janey, this is an official visit —”

“I was afraid it might be. Tomorrow.”

She drove Elliot home, dropped off the movies the boys had rented, and went home to bed and tried not to think about sex.

She would love to have invited Mel over for the night, but that would violate her own rules. She didn’t believe in having an affair in the same house her kids were in. Not that they didn’t know the nature of the relationship — well, Todd seemed unaware that Mel was anything more than Mom’s friend. Katie understood, but doggedly pretended not to, which left her in the difficult position of having to both ignore and disapprove of the same thing. Only Mike seemed okay with it. Jane knew her attitude was stodgy and priggish, but she couldn’t help it. And she suspected that Mel, while he claimed to be perplexed by her attitude, didn’t truly relish the idea of making love to her in the same bed she’d shared with her husband.

In the morning, she left the still-sleeping kids a note and sat down on the front porch to wait for Mel. When he drove up, she went straight to his little red MG and hopped in. "You look great," he said.

She had a new summer dress Shelley had forced her to buy. It was an old-fashioned white eyelet fabric lined with a pale blue fabric, and had a rather naked bodice held up by spaghetti straps. "I'd look like a beached albino whale in that!" Jane had said when Shelley whipped the dress off the rack and held it up.

"No, you'll look great. Tan is out these days," Shelley had assured her. "And you can wear a nice lacy summer sweater with it if you want."

Apparently Shelley had been right. As usual.

"Thanks, Mel. I feel like I'm going around in public in a nightgown, but Shelley assures me I'm stylish. You look good, too."

They went to a restaurant a few miles away that specialized in fancy brunches. Jane managed to put away most of a mushroom and artichoke omelet without spilling anything on herself. Mel knocked back eggs, bacon, toast, hash browns, grilled tomatoes, an enormous sweet roll, two glasses of orange juice, and coffee. "If I ate that much, you'd have to roll me home," Jane complained.

They chatted about various harmless subjects while they ate — the graduation, Mike's new truck, and their plans for a weekend in Wisconsin later in the month. They were very careful not to talk about the recent deaths. When they left the restaurant, Mel drove to a nearby park where they could speak privately. Mel got out, removed a briefcase from the trunk of the car, and sat back down to rummage for a moment among the papers inside. He handed Jane a photocopy of a typed sheet.

"Take a look," he said.

She skimmed it quickly. "It's notes from the time I talked to Stonecipher about setting up trusts for my kids," she said, giving it back.

"And this one?" He gave her another photocopy. This was handwritten. And the sketchy phrases were about Jane's late husband — his date of death, his involvement in the family pharmacy business, his income. There were notes about Thelma, including a few rash, if not downright insulting, remarks Jane had made about her. And another about the pharmacy having difficulties with the IRS with the comment, "Fraud?" underlined.

Jane felt herself grow hot and uncomfortable. She gave the paper back to Mel, even though what she wanted to do was crumple it and throw it away.

Mel put it back in the briefcase. "The first sheet was from your file in Stonecipher's office. The official file. The second was in a folder in Emma Weyrich's bedroom."

Jane felt leaden. "Emma's bedroom? Why did she have it?" she asked finally.

"I think she intended to talk to you about it. At your four o'clock appointment."

"Why?"

Mel looked at her for a long moment. "I think she considered you blackmailable."

"Me? But why? Because I made a few cranky cracks about my mother-in-law? Or because that jerk thought the Jeffry family was cheating on their taxes? Fraud! The nerve of him. It was just a fight over allowable deductions, which the company won eventually. There was no question of fraud."

"She didn't know that. And wouldn't have until she spoke to you about it. When she approached you after the graduation ceremony, she didn't mention your husband or his family, did she?"

"No, of course not. She just summoned me."

"You're positive of that?"

Jane bridled. “I told you so. Before she died, in fact.”

He took her hand. “I’m sorry, Janey. I warned you this was official.”

“Are you saying I’m a suspect in her death, Detective VanDyne?” she snapped, pulling her hand away.

“No, I’m saying you’re not. You see, this was in a folder. Like this one,” he added, taking a brand-new file folder out of the briefcase. It was a hanging-type file, with two light metal bars. “This handwritten sheet was in a blue one. The only fingerprints on it were Stonecipher’s and Weyrich’s. Not yours.”

“But this folder was by itself and the police think she was trying to blackmail me with the contents? If she had talked to me about the contents, I wouldn’t have necessarily even seen the thing, much less touched it,” she said grimly.

He nodded and said, “Right, but look at the file folder. See where there is a row across the top of these prepunched vertical slots that you pop out to insert a label?” He demonstrated, pushing his thumb against one of the dozen or so spots. A little lozenge of the blue card-stock fell out.

“Yes. So?”

"So when my people combed the apartment, they found a yellow piece like this in the sofa cushions and a red one stuck up against the leg of the coffee table. Watch —" He gave the top of the folder a slight twist and another little blue lozenge fell out into his lap.

"Oh —" Jane said, the light dawning. "Other folders."

"Right. Other folders that weren't in the apartment when we searched it. I'm just speculating here, but I think the scenario was this: She brought certain folders home from the office — these were in a separate file drawer in Stonecipher's desk, by the way, not with the official filing system. She probably had them in her bedroom and brought them out to the living room one at a time."

"Are you saying she had a whole list of people she'd ordered to come over?"

"Not saying," he said firmly. "Speculating. There's a world of difference. But there apparently are at least two others who might have been in the apartment. The ones with the red folder and the yellow folder."

"But the folders were no longer in her apartment? Or did you find them?"

"Nope. Gone. Possibly scooped up and

taken by the person who killed her."

"So the fact that the folder about me was still there —"

"Pretty much lets you off the hook. At least as far as I'm concerned," Mel replied.

Jane thought for a minute. "So there was a whole file drawer of these in Stonecipher's office?"

Mel looked grim. "Afraid so. In a locked drawer in his desk. Emma had the key in her purse."

"Do you mean in addition to being a full-fledged bastard, the guy was a blackmailer, too?" Jane asked angrily.

"Now, now. Calm down. Let's say he was a potential blackmailer. The drawer full of files might have just been a hedge against inflation. He never approached you after your one visit, did he?"

"Good Lord, no! In fact, he never acted like he even remembered who I was. But then, all he had on me was something mildly embarrassing. What other kinds of things were left behind in the file drawer? I don't mean specifics —"

"Mostly fairly innocuous stuff," Mel said. "But there were a few pretty hot items."

"Then why were they still in the file drawer?" Jane asked. "That doesn't make sense. Why would Emma pull out something silly and trivial about me and leave something juicy in the file?"

"Because the 'juicy' stuff, as you put it, was about people who aren't around anymore. At least the ones we've been able to check so far. They've moved away or died or — in one case — already gone to jail for the transgression mentioned in the file."

"Mel, I'm not following this. You apparently have some theory. I hate to be stupid, but —"

"No, it's not you. I'm being deliberately vague, wondering if you'd leap to the same conclusion I did. Which is something I shouldn't be doing — forming theories without enough facts. You see, it has to do with what's *not* in the file drawer. When I interviewed everybody I could find who attended the deli opening, I turned up several people who had dealings with Stonecipher at one time or another. Like the Dohertys just as an example — the people who got the nasty divorce and then got back together and didn't have any money left because Stonecipher had cleaned them out."

"And there wasn't a file for them?" Jane asked. "I'm sorry, but that doesn't necessarily mean anything except that he didn't know anything nasty about them."

Mel cocked an eyebrow. "After representing an angry wife in a prolonged, ugly divorce suit, he had nothing to the husband's disadvantage?"

"Hmm. I see what you mean. LeAnne probably said some pretty nasty things about Charles. And true or not, he probably kept a record since he was given to doing that sort of thing."

Mel put the folder back in the briefcase. "That's what I thought, too. So I got out my list of interviews from the deli opening, pulled out those names of people who admitted to having consulted Stonecipher. I checked those names against the private files and found practically none of them. Now, as you said, that could mean he just didn't have anything on them. Or —"

"— or it could mean those were the other files Emma pulled out," Jane finished.

Mel shut the briefcase and leaned back, rubbing his eyes with the palms of his hands. "And it's all a theory. With nothing to back it up. In fact, the whole theory's based on what's *not* there. The dog that didn't bark."

They sat in silence for a long time and Mel finally opened his door. "Want to walk?"

"Think it will make my brain work?" Jane said with a smile.

"Your mind doesn't have to work on this. Mine does. I only told you this because it involved you in a way."

He came around and helped her out. After locking the car, he took her hand and started strolling toward the swing set at the far end of the park.

"How do you suppose Emma knew about the private files?" Jane asked as they walked.

"She contributed," Mel replied. "They were two of a kind, her and her sleazy boss. She was his paralegal, did some initial interviews and such. Some of the notes are in her handwriting."

"Because she thought someday he'd dump his wife, marry her, and the two of them would settle down to a nice little blackmailing racket in their golden years," Jane said, disgusted.

"Maybe. We'll never know. They're both dead."

"Good!" Jane said. "Sorry. I shouldn't have said that, but it sure doesn't sound like either of them will be missed. But couldn't he have already been using the material he'd accumulated?"

"Could be."

"Which might explain why some people didn't fight him on his various 'causes.' He might have used what he knew to make people knuckle under instead of trying to get money from them," Jane mused.

"That's possible," Mel said. "We'll have experts go over all his books with a fine-tooth comb to see if there's any extra money unaccounted for, but it will take a while."

Jane sat down on a swing and Mel went around behind her, putting his hands on her shoulders and pushing her gently.

"You know," Jane said, "I can see him doing that — making people go along with his nutty causes by reminding them of their sins — and feeling very noble about it," Jane said. "He was a ends-justify-the-means kind of person. He wouldn't have cared, I imagine, how many people he made miserable so long as he got his damned bicycle lane or fat content on menus."

Mel just rubbed her shoulders and said, "Mmm."

"Do you think that's why somebody pushed the rack over on him? Just because they were so damned glad to find him dead and a bunch of old anger boiled up?"

"I've wandered too far from facts and

into theory already," Mel said. "And I need to get back to work on the facts. Ready to go home?"

"I guess so," Jane said. "I'd rather stay here and swing though."

"So would I," he said, bending to plant a light kiss on her bare shoulder. "But duty calls."

When they got to Jane's house, Mel said, "Don't talk to anyone about all this."

"Shelley — ?"

"Oh, she could probably read your mind anyway, but don't talk to anybody else and for God's sake, don't try to help by snooping."

"Okay. I wish I could read my own mind," Jane said as he helped her out of the car. She'd plucked one of the little blue lozenges of paper off her skirt and was staring at it.

— 13 —

Shelley must have seen her come home because the phone started ringing the minute Jane opened the kitchen door. "You looked smashing!" Shelley said. "Bet Mel was knocked out."

"Huh? Oh, the dress. Yes."

"So, what did he say? Not about the dress. About Emma."

"Tons. Bizarre stuff. And I even have permission to tell you. But I have to get to the grocery store before the kids and animals start gnawing on the furniture."

"Hang up the dress first."

"Yes, Mother!" Jane said, laughing.

Jane was back in an hour, the station wagon practically dragging from the weight of the groceries. Shelley met her in the driveway and carried in a bag of ice. Jane grabbed a bag and bellowed for the kids to carry in the rest. Only Todd showed up. "He must be the hungriest," Jane muttered.

Shelley helped put things away as they came in. "My God! I hope you had lots of coupons along. What did you do, buy one of everything in the store?"

"Nearly. I'm determined not to go back for at least two weeks, except for bread or milk. Leave all the meats on the corner of the counter until I figure out which I want to cook first and I'll put the rest in the basement freezer."

"Eight packages of Jell-O? Have you lost your mind?"

"Todd could live on it," Jane said, taking a couple nearly empty cereal boxes out of an upper cabinet in order to put new ones in. She dumped all the old cereal into one box, put it back in the cabinet and went to the bottom of the stairs to bellow up, "Mike, come get Willard's food out of the car. The bag's too heavy for Todd to carry."

"So what did Mel have to say?" Shelley asked as she folded empty grocery bags.

"A lot, but it's sort of baroque and I have to concentrate to even tell it right. Wait a minute until the kids are out from underfoot."

Mike slumped through the kitchen and was back in a minute with a fifty-pound bag of dog food on his shoulder. He made some Tarzan noises as he passed them on his way to the basement.

When he returned, Shelley said to him, "I want a ride in the truck pretty soon."

He snagged a carton of milk Jane was putting away, grabbed a glass, and hitched his chair up to the table. "Tell you what, Mrs. Nowack, why don't you and Mom go somewhere in it this evening? Scott and I are double-dating and have to use his car."

"That sounds great. You'd really trust us with it?"

"Well, I've a rope tied to it to pull you back if you go more than a mile, but yeah," Mike said, grinning.

Jane finished putting away the food, leaving out bread, jelly, sliced ham, lettuce, mayo, and peanut butter for the kids to fix sandwiches. "No chips?" Katie wailed as she came into the kitchen.

"Cabinet next to the oven," Jane said. "Have you *never* noticed where they live?"

A little later, sitting on the patio with Shelley, she was still grousing. "Of course she doesn't know where I keep anything because she never troubles to put anything away. But I had a shock yesterday. She cleaned up her room. *Without being told to.*"

"That's scary!" Shelley said. "Maybe you're about to enter a new era. Tell me what Mel said."

Jane took a deep breath, reviewed it in her head for a second, and launched into a long monologue full of "he saids" and "I saids." Shelley listened quietly, occasionally saying, "Wait. Wait. Let me think." Then, "Okay, go ahead."

When Jane was done, Shelley said, "What a pair they were! Using and either abusing or planning to abuse the client privilege. Do you think they'd already been using the material they had to blackmail people?"

Jane thought for a minute. "You know, if I had to guess, I'd say not. I think if Stonecipher had been using it, he'd have gotten more cooperation in ramming through his silly rules. He's lost on practically all his causes, hasn't he?"

"I think so. But that's assuming he'd blackmail people for moral support rather than plain old cash. And he appeared to have lots and lots of money. Those house renovations alone must have run well over $100,000 apart from the decorating. And you saw those Oriental rugs in the living room. I don't think they came from Sears. The real things cost the earth."

"Even the fake ones are out of my range. Can't you just picture Weyrich and Stonecipher staying late at the office, poring over their nasty little private file cabinet?" Jane shuddered. "That's really creepy."

"So Mel gave the Dohertys as an example of people who were at the deli opening, had dealt with Stonecipher, and didn't have a file. Did he mention anyone else?"

"No. I don't think he was suggesting they were high on his list of suspects, though. Just giving an example that I'd recognize because we were the ones who blabbed to him about them."

"I'd sure like to see his short list," Shelley said.

"So would I, but if you think I'm going to ask —"

"God, no! He'd be down on us like a ton of bricks," Shelley agreed.

"Stay here a minute," Jane said and went inside.

She came back out with the little blue lozenge of cardstock from the file folder. "Does that look familiar to you?"

Shelley stuck out her hand and Jane put the paper on her palm. "I don't think so," Shelley replied. "Why?"

"Because it rings a terribly faint bell in the back of my mind."

"Maybe you've had file folders like it."

"Maybe. It could be that I've vacuumed

up bits like this. But I don't think so."

"Close your eyes and try to picture where you've seen it," Shelley advised.

"I've tried that. I can't bring it any farther forward in my mind."

"Maybe that time you were in Stonecipher's office — ?" Shelley handed the bit of paper back and Jane put it in her jeans pocket.

"No, if I really have seen such a thing before, it's been much more recent. But I don't think it was blue. If I could get a fix on the color, I might be able — oh, well. Never mind. I'm probably mixing it up in my head with something else entirely."

"Poor Mel. He's really up a creek, isn't he?" Shelley said. "The dog that didn't bark. I like that phrase. It's from a Sherlock Holmes story, isn't it?"

"I wonder how many people she had lined up," Jane said. "If she wanted to see me at four, that probably means she had at least the two people who belonged to the red and yellow file before me. And who knows how many others?"

"What a cold-blooded bitch," Shelley said.

"Yes, but in a way I feel sorry for her. Not just because she's dead, but because of what Patsy Mallett said about the argument she overheard. Emma wasn't a kid anymore. She must have been — what? — thirty-five or so? She might have been hanging in there being the other woman for a large part of her adult life. And then, when Rhonda said she was divorcing Stonecipher, Emma thought she was going to get the big payoff. Instead, he apparently told her he had no intention of marrying her. Think of the blow to her ego that must have been."

"Not only her ego, but her finances," Shelley added.

"Yes. I hadn't thought about it that way, but she'd been counting on being his wife some day and having financial security and she had it yanked out from under her. I can almost see why she'd act so quickly and probably angrily to cash in on that file drawer full of dirty little secrets."

"I don't suppose there was any kind of index in the file drawer?"

"I doubt it," Jane said. "And I imagine if there had been, Mel would have mentioned it. How's he going to tell what's missing when he has no way of knowing what was there?"

"Well, he has his list of people who admitted having consulted Stonecipher. That's a start."

"But doesn't prove anything. Most people don't go to see a lawyer and immediately pour out all their most heartfelt secrets and/or criminal activities," Jane said.

"Still, you don't go to a lawyer unless you have a problem of some kind. And most problems are, to some degree or another, your own fault. Even if it's just failing to have done something you should have."

"Mom?" a distant voice bellowed.

"Out in back," Jane bellowed back.

Mike came out the garage door. "You forgot orange juice."

"No, I didn't. I got it. Look in the fridge."

"I did. And on the counters and even in the car. It's on the receipt, but it didn't get home," Mike said.

"Phooey! The sacker must have left it out. And I guess you can't live without it?"

"I'll drive you to the store, Jane," Shelley offered. "I need to pick something up anyway."

"So much for not going shopping for another two weeks," Jane complained. "I didn't even make it for two hours."

She went in and got her purse and they took off. Jane's gallon of orange juice was still sitting at the checkout she'd gone through, waiting for her to come back. The clerk didn't even want to see her receipt. Shelley went off to find the cream cheese she needed for a recipe she was trying out and Jane waited in front of the store.

And waited.

She finally got impatient and went back into the store to find Shelley. Reaching the dairy case, she discovered Shelley in conversation with LeAnne Doherty. Shelley gave Jane an I wondered-when-you'd-get-here look.

"Hi, Jane. Sorry I wasn't in the shop yesterday when you stopped by," LeAnne said.

LeAnne was a plump, pretty woman in her thirties with naturally curly reddish hair and freckles. She still had on her church clothes and a grocery cart full of mostly house brands. A careful shopper, Jane thought.

"Oh, we just wanted to say hi, nothing important," Jane said.

"You've heard about Emma Weyrich, I guess," LeAnne said, lowering her voice.

"We have," Shelley said neutrally. "Awful, isn't it?"

"Are you still dating that detective, Jane?" LeAnne asked.

"Uh-huh," Jane said warily.

"I guess he tells you all about his cases."

"Afraid not," Jane said.

"Is he investigating Emma's death?" LeAnne asked, undeterred.

Jane saw no reason for concealment. "Yes, he is."

"How was she killed? This morning's paper just said a blow to the head."

"Some kind of barbell thing, I think," Jane replied. That, too, would soon be public information if it wasn't already.

"I guess they went over her apartment pretty carefully," LeAnne said. "I wonder if they found anything — helpful."

Jane shrugged. "I have no idea. I know they search really thoroughly."

"So you don't know what they found?"

"Me? No. Mel wouldn't even consider sharing inside information with me," Jane lied. *I wish he were here,* Jane thought. *He'd be impressed. And very interested in LeAnne's questions.*

"It must be really interesting dating a detective," LeAnne said in a terribly perky tone.

"It's weird to be dating at all," Jane said.

"I know! When Charles and I were separated, I dated a bit and it was strange. My ice cream's melting. I guess I better run along. Nice visiting with you." On this almost hysterically chirpy note, she wheeled her cart away hurriedly.

Shelley said, "Do you suppose she thought she was being subtle?"

"Did you see her hands?" Jane asked. "She was clutching the handle of the grocery cart so hard I expected it to crumple."

"The only thing her questions didn't tell us was which color folder was hers," Shelley said.

"Poor LeAnne," Jane said. "She probably had one an inch thick. Think of all the dirt she must have dished about Charles during the divorce."

"But Jane, could anybody as pathetically unsubtle as LeAnne commit an actual murder and manage to even get out of the room without giving herself away? After the performance we just saw, I can imagine her running out in the hallway and looking for people to tell, 'You haven't seen me here, have you?' "

Jane laughed. "There would have to be a huge amount of evidence to convince me she could carry it off. Still, for as silly as she was just being, there's more to her than that. Just look at the dedication and determination it's taken for them to pull themselves out of bankruptcy and get a whole new business started? Not to mention the intelligence it takes. It can't be all Charles's doing."

"Sure it could," Shelley said, picking up the cream cheese she'd come in for and moving toward the checkout. "And maybe that's what she's afraid of. That Charles was the one Emma had an appointment with."

Jane fell silent while Shelley made her purchase. Once they were back in the car, she said, "You could be right, you know. I hardly know Charles, do you?"

Shelley shrugged. "No. Paul had some dealings with him years ago when Charles was still with that investment company or mortgage company, whatever it was." Shelley's husband, Paul, was, among other things, the owner of a chain of Greek fast-food restaurants that he'd started from scratch.

"What did Paul think of him?"

"He said Charles was bright and ambitious enough, but didn't seem to think he was spectacular in any way. A nice guy. I'll ask him again, but I doubt he'll have much more to add. It was about the land for one of the restaurant franchises and I think they met only once or twice over some routine details. Not a situation where you'd get to know someone intimately."

Jane nodded. "Shelley, would Paul have any special insights into the deli's business?"

"He might, but it doesn't seem to have anything much to do with the deli anymore, does it?"

"I don't think so, but who knows? Conrad and Sarah have led a pretty strange life and Stonecipher might have known something about them, too."

"How could he? They only came back here recently and as soon as they did, they started the deli and he started his zoning war. It's not likely they ever considered being clients of his."

"True. But maybe he dug up something about their past when he was trying to shut them down. Drugs or something? They lived a pretty hippie-dippy life for a long time according to Grace. Maybe they didn't pay their taxes or something like that."

"Yes, but if he had anything on them, wouldn't he have used it to apply pressure on them before the deli could open?" Shelley asked.

"I guess you're right. He really did pull out all the stops to try to keep them from opening."

Shelley started the van. "I feel like a rat

in a maze that hasn't any opening. Every time I think about this, I end up at the same dead end."

"Which is?"

"Stonecipher's death," Shelley said, backing out ruthlessly and ignoring the uproar of honking this caused. "It's too coincidental that both Stonecipher and Emma would die under suspicious circumstances without there being a connection. But why would anybody want to make a natural death look like a murder?"

— 14 —

They'd gone only two blocks when Jane noticed a car at the side of the street. The hood was up and an older man was looking into the engine. "Hold it, Shelley," Jane said. "Isn't that Foster Hanlon? Let's stop and help. We might pry something interesting out of him."

"I'd like to pry the old bastard's guts out of him," Shelley said.

"Come on, Shelley. You can stand a few minutes. Keep in mind that he was with Stonecipher at the deli. Right on his heels."

Grumbling, Shelley pulled over and backed up, and the two of them got out of the van. Hanlon was a small, wiry man who could have been anywhere from sixty to eighty years old. He had thinning yellow-white hair; a stiff, erect carriage that was almost military; and a face that was a road map of fine wrinkles. He was dressed in a dark three-piece suit with a white shirt so heavily starched it probably crackled when he moved.

"Mr. Hanlon, have you got engine problems?" Jane asked.

He straightened up so quickly that he bumped his head on the hood. "Oh, yes. Well, I think so. I'm sorry to admit that not only do I know very little about cars, but I don't even know who you are."

It was, on the surface, a reasonable, inoffensive sentence, but Jane found it obnoxious. She was tempted to say, "Oh, we're just a couple neighborhood muggers, stopped to beat and rob you." Shelley's grim expression hinted that she was thinking along the same lines.

"I'm Jane Jeffry and this is Shelley Nowack. Do you need —"

"Jeffry. Jeffry? Oh, yes. The house with the driveway that needs repairing," Hanlon said. "And Mrs. Nowack is next door. You could use a bit of paint on the trim around your windows, Mrs. Nowack."

"And you —" Shelley began.

Jane elbowed her and said, "I don't know anything about engines either, but we'd be glad to give you a lift to a service station. *Wouldn't we, Shelley?*"

"Oh, of course," Shelley replied with dangerous cheerfulness. "By way of the nearest sheer cliff," she finished under her breath.

"I — well, what I really need is a lift home. I've got groceries in the car that are melting. If you wouldn't really mind."

"Not at all," Jane said. "We'll just help you put them in the back of the van."

He had a surprising number of grocery sacks, including one holding two bags of ice that were already beginning to drip. "Mrs. Nowack, you are aware of the speed limit here, aren't you?" he said as Shelley took off like a rocket.

She slammed on the brakes, flinging him forward. "Oh, I must have forgotten for a moment," she said sweetly. "You didn't get hurt, did you?"

The rest of the way, he acted like a demented tour guide. "There's an example of neglect," he said. "Perfectly sound house but the cracks in the foundation are just being patched instead of getting to the real problem. And over there. That yard is a disgrace. There are more dandelions than grass. No excuse for it. Causes grief for all the neighbors who keep their lawns nice. It's not that much trouble. Just mowing, seeding, fertilizing, weed killer, occasional de-thatching — the neighborhood association has a nice pamphlet on proper lawn care for anybody who needs it. I keep a stack of them in the car and drop them off to people when I see their lawns suffering neglect."

"I wonder," Shelley said dreamily, "if anybody has done studies on a possible connection between neighborhood associations and the neo-Nazi movement?"

This remark seemed to genuinely puzzle him and he was quiet for a bit.

Jane leaned forward on the pretense of finding something on the radio and whispered to Shelley, "We're trying to find out about a murder, not commit one!"

His house was just what Jane would have expected. It was an oversized Cape Cod, immaculately kept. The windows gleamed as if polished only moments before. The paint almost looked as if it were still wet. The lawn was lush jade-green and still showed the tidy diagonal mowing marks. You could have eaten off the driveway. A row of neat forsythia bushes bordered both sides of the lot separating him from his neighbors. They'd been trimmed into tortuous cubes of precisely the same size.

"Let me take this ice inside for you," Jane said. She was determined they wouldn't just drop him off and go on their way. Shelley understood and sulkily picked through the bags in the back of the van for the lightest one.

The inside of the house matched the outside. It wasn't stark, in fact there were a lot of pictures, ornaments, and furniture, but everything was so clean, fresh, and geometric that it seemed unreal, as if it had been created on a computer. The sofa in the living room was precisely positioned in front of the empty, spotless fireplace in which there had obviously never been anything so sloppy and uncontrolled as a fire. Two matching chairs sat at exact right angles. A stack of *National Geographics* on the coffee table were in date order and each was offset an inch and a half from the others.

Jane wondered if there was a wife who went along with this and had the vague recollection of having heard that Foster Hanlon was a widower. She took the bags of ice to the sink, punched a hole in the bottom of each to drain out the melted water, and opened the freezer door. There, not surprisingly, banks of frozen vegetable packages were neatly stacked. She was afraid to look too closely for fear of finding that they were actually in alphabetical order.

"Go ahead and call the service station," Shelley said. "We can put this away for you," she added with a gleam in her eye.

Hanlon looked disconcerted by this upheaval in his tidy life, as well he should. The moment he left the kitchen, Shelley set a package of cereal in with the canned goods and added a package of paper napkins before closing the door with satisfaction. It would take him all day to get everything back the way he wanted it.

When he was through phoning, Jane and Shelley had everything put away. Somewhere. "They're picking me up in about ten minutes," he said.

"Oh, good," Jane said cheerfully. She settled in at the kitchen table with a vacuous expression. "It's been an unusual week for you, hasn't it? For all of us, really."

"Has it? In what way?" he asked, reluctantly sitting down across from her. Shelley took the chair between them.

"Well, with Robert Stonecipher's death and then Emma's."

"Emma?" he asked.

"Emma Weyrich. His assistant," Jane said. "Hadn't you heard?"

"No, I'm sorry, but I don't even recognize the name," he said.

"Surely you knew her," Shelley said. "She came to the deli with you and Mr. Stonecipher."

"I went to the deli opening on my own,"

he said firmly. "Oh, that athletic young woman. Is that who you mean? What happened to her?"

"She was murdered," Jane said. Surely someone as nosy as he must know this.

"Oh?" he asked. "Where?"

"In her apartment," Jane said, curious why he'd asked the question.

"Oh, well — an apartment resident," he said. "I've never approved of apartments in good residential areas. It brings in the aimless, irresponsible element of society. When you aren't a property owner, your interest in the welfare of the community is seriously diminished."

Jane and Shelley gawked at him. Jane was the first to recover. And to steer the conversation in a different, potentially more useful direction. "I don't see how you could not know who she was. After all, she was Stonecipher's assistant. You and he must have worked pretty closely together on the zoning . . ." She fumbled for a word other than "outrage" and could only come up with "thing."

"I wouldn't say we worked together. We had a common interest in that particular problem, naturally, as should the whole neighborhood," he said, apparently offended. "But Mr. Stonecipher and I were certainly not close friends or frequent companions."

Shelley raised an eyebrow. "So you didn't like him much?"

"No, I didn't say that," he said carefully. "It was merely that we had only a few, very specific things in common. Like the problem of the deli. Unfortunately, he had a most unpleasant personality."

"Did he?" Jane asked. "I hardly knew him at all. What was he like?"

"Very opinionated —" Foster Hanlon said.

Jane nudged Shelley with her knee to keep her from exploding.

"— and unwilling to listen to other views," Hanlon went on. "In fact, I had rather strong words with him over his proposal to put in bicycle lanes. He felt strongly about it, of course, but was blind to the fact that it would have been terribly expensive to widen the roads and repave them. It would have meant condemning a few feet of property along the entire length of the routes he proposed. The way the city code is drawn up in regard to benefit districts, it would have raised taxes so that the very people who were losing their land would have ended up paying for the loss."

Shelley said, “I presume this street was one of the ones he wanted to widen.”

“Yes, but that’s not the point!” he said defensively.

“He lost that battle, didn’t he?” Jane said.

This soothed Hanlon. “Yes, I’m glad to say he did. But I believe it was only a temporary setback. He would have brought it up again, I feel certain. Do you know, I heard he was planning to propose that the city council be increased in number and was going to try to get some of his adherents on. Sort of like”— he lowered his voice as if uttering an obscenity — “Roosevelt trying to pack the Supreme Court.”

“How interesting,” Jane said. “Where did you hear that?”

He replied warily. “I don’t recall exactly. Several people mentioned it to me.”

Jane had a sudden bizarre vision of groups of neighbors holding secret meetings in a deserted farmhouse at night to think up false rumors to pass along to Foster Hanlon just to drive him crazy. Driving dark cars and wearing trenchcoats. Meeting by candlelight with the windows covered. Speaking in whispers. The image tickled her and she couldn’t help but smile.

Hanlon glared at her. "You find this amusing?"

"No, no. I'm sorry. I was thinking about something else entirely," Jane said. "So you didn't come to the deli opening with Mr. Stonecipher?"

"No, I didn't." He kept glancing at his watch nervously, hoping for someone to rescue him, Jane assumed.

"Why did you go at all?" Shelley asked.

He drew himself up. "It was, I believe, a public event. I was as entitled to come as anyone else."

"Of course. But why did you want to go?" Shelley persisted.

"To see if the zoning regulations and health codes were being observed," he said. He seemed proud, rather than ashamed, of himself. "This dreadful intrusion of a retail business in a residential neighborhood could be catastrophic to our property values. Yours and mine! And they're not even respectable people."

"Who's not respectable? What do you mean by that," Jane said, her amusement fading.

"The Bakers. They're hippies. That's what I mean. Oh, yes. They started out here, but they didn't absorb any of the family values of the community."

"Excuse me?" Shelley said.

Anybody else would have backed off at her tone, but Hanlon plowed on. "They're just fly-by-nights. No permanent home until they came here. You mark my words, they'll soon trash that place and trash the whole neighborhood. Pretty soon they'll start hiring blacks and Mexicans and —"

Shelley suddenly stood up and headed for the front door. "I'm sorry, Jane. This is all I can take."

Jane was right behind her, with Hanlon bringing up the rear, making insincere remarks of gratitude for the lift home mixed up with further warnings about property values and the shortsightedness of people who made no effort to protect their investments.

The two women leaped into the van and sped off.

"I feel like I need to soak in a vat of disinfectant," Shelley said when she pulled into her driveway. "I've already thought of at least sixteen really nasty things to say to him and I'd like to drive straight back there and say them all."

"And none of them would make the slightest difference," Jane said sadly.

"No. A bigot is a bigot is a bigot. Ugh! What a thoroughly, bone-deep nasty person he is. Why did you make us do that?"

"To see if we could learn anything, of course."

"Did we?" Shelley asked with disgust. "Anything we wanted to know?"

Jane thought for a minute. "Only that he wasn't great chums with Stonecipher —"

"The man's never been chums with anyone. Who could stand him for more than five minutes?"

"— and that he didn't seem to know who Emma Weyrich was."

Shelley waved this away, still furious. "Come on, Jane, if you thought you could get away with pretending you didn't even know her, wouldn't you? Not you, of course, but if you were he?"

"That's a hideous thought. Being him," Jane said.

— 15 —

Shelley arrived at six-thirty for her ride in Mike's truck. Mike had to show them how everything worked, as if they weren't capable of figuring it out themselves. "Where are we going?" Shelley asked when they pulled out of the driveway.

"There are a couple houses over in the fancy new subdivision just to the west open today. If it's not too late, I thought we might go gawk," Jane replied.

"Thinking of moving?" Shelley asked with a laugh.

"No way on earth. But I like to torture myself with the idea of clean closets and new kitchens. No, the only way I'd leave my house is on a gurney. You know, I cleaned out the upstairs hall closet last week. Took every single thing out, threw half of it away, and the half I kept wouldn't fit back in. What bizarre law of physics makes closets that way?"

"I don't know. But I've experienced it myself. Things seem to fluff up just by being taken out and handled. Somebody's probably got a million-dollar government grant to study it as we speak."

They stopped at a light, and a car full of teenagers pulled up next to them, admiring the truck and laughing hysterically at the incongruity of the middle-aged passengers. "Feel a little silly?" Shelley asked Jane.

"Wait until we get to the show house and the realtor runs around turning off lights and locking the doors," Jane said with a grin.

They were too late and doors were already locked and lights off when they arrived, so they contented themselves with driving around looking at the outsides of the new homes and imagining what wonders might be within.

"I've been thinking all afternoon about that old jerk Hanlon," Shelley confessed as they stopped in front of an enormous house with elaborate landscaping. "Imagine still holding a grudge against Roosevelt more than half a century later. That's world-class rancor. I want to know what you were grinning about like a Cheshire cat while he was ranting."

Jane told her about her vision of neighbors meeting to think up rumors to upset him. "An abandoned hunting lodge, way out in the country. I think," she said, giggling.

Shelley laughed. "A special knock and a password. Like 'New Deal.' "

" 'Long live the NRA,' " Jane suggested with a laugh.

"I hate to admit it, but as much as I'd like to see Foster Hanlon blamed for almost anything," Shelley said, "I can't believe he was responsible for Emma's death. Or even the business of pushing the rack over on Stonecipher. Both of those events were messy. And Hanlon's too fastidious to be involved in anything messy."

Jane had been studying the lawn of the house they were parked in front of while Shelley talked. "And they both took a bit of strength. Not a lot, but he seems so frail. No, I think if he were going to kill someone, he'd just talk to them until they had a stroke out of sheer frustration."

"Interesting, though, that he made no bones about not liking Stonecipher."

"Oh, he speaks his mind, all right. I think he's so used to people being offended by what he says that it would never cross his mind that he might actually endanger himself with his opinions. Imagine going through life with people looking shocked or offended or edging away from you every time you expressed one of your opinions. Wouldn't you catch on eventually that your opinions were pretty nasty?"

"I don't think people like him care," Shelley said. "They're so convinced that they're right. There's a sort of reforming zeal that appears to motivate them. He probably imagines that they are shocked when he speaks because they'd never thought about it from his view and are going to go home and change their ways, thanks to him."

"But he must not have any friends at all."

"Oh, I'm sure he does. Other awful people who agree with him that the world is going to hell in a handbasket and if people would only listen to them, everything would be okay. It would only take a couple others like that to make you feel you were part of a very special, select group. In fact, their very exclusivity probably appeals to them."

Jane sighed. "I guess so. But it's so depressing. Shelley, how would you ever mow this lawn? Look at the slope of it."

"If you could afford to live here, you could afford gardeners. Or a flock of sheep, for that matter. Hey! Let's start a rumor that we're going to get sheep to do our lawns!" She rummaged in her purse for a piece of gum, then started to put the wrapper in the ashtray. "No, I can't be the first to sully a pristine ashtray."

"There's a paper bag on the floor," Jane said. "See what's in that."

Shelley picked it up and looked. "Trash. Good." She popped the gum wrapper in. "Isn't that nice that he's keeping it so clean?"

"I give it a week," Jane said.

They headed back home, where Mike met them in the driveway. He must have been watching for them from the front window. "How'd you like it? Doesn't it drive great?" he said, and tried casually to look at the odometer to see how far they'd gone.

"Great, Mike. Has a lot of power out on the highway," Jane said. "It doesn't even shimmy until you get up to about a hundred and ten miles an hour."

He rolled his eyes. "Yeah, sure, Mom. Like you've ever gone over fifty-five."

"What are you doing here?" Jane asked. "I thought you and Scott were double-dating."

"Yeah, but I asked him to pick me up last so I could see what you thought of the truck."

"So you could see when I brought it back, you mean," Jane said, smiling. Then to Shelley: "That low, rumbling sound you hear is the generations rolling over."

"Hey, Mom, you won't care if I put the truck in the garage and leave the station wagon out, will you?" Mike asked, polishing off an invisible spot on the hood with his shirt tail.

"Oh, no. Not at all. About sixteen more raindrops and the station wagon will become one hundred percent rust and just be an orange spot on the driveway. Maybe I could park it over the pothole and the nondegradable bits will fill in the hole."

"Does that mean no?" Mike asked.

"That's what it means. If you'd clean out the other half of the garage, you could park it there."

"Mom! The other half of the garage is full of junk."

"Yes, and you now have the ideal vehicle for taking it all to the dump," Jane said. "Shelley, can you come in?"

"After I tell Paul I'm home."

Jane went inside, carrying Mike's small paper sack of trash. The phone was ringing. She reached for it seconds before Katie raced into the kitchen and skidded to a stop.

"Janey, have you had dinner?" Mel asked.

"Not exactly. Want to come over for a sandwich? I pillaged the grocery store."

"I thought you'd never ask. Five minutes," he said.

He and Shelley arrived at the same time. Jane had dragged out sandwich stuff, to which Mel applied himself as if he hadn't eaten in days. The women waited as patiently as they could for him to finish eating, telling him about their visit with Foster Hanlon.

The minute he swallowed his last bite of sandwich, Jane said, "So how's the investigation of Emma's death going?"

"Got any cookies?" he asked. She produced two different packages of store-bought pastries. "A nightmare," he said, picking an oatmeal-raisin cookie and getting up to pour himself a glass of milk. "There was an open house two doors down from Weyrich's apartment from eleven to two. Somebody's retirement party. All sorts of people up and down the hallway. And a couple next to her on the other side had a garageless garage sale going on until three. That hallway must have looked like a couple of great ethnic migrations colliding. About all I've got is two more long lists of names with a few that overlap with the deli opening list and are probably pure coincidence."

"Nobody saw anyone going into Emma's apartment?" Jane asked.

"Quite the contrary. A lot of them saw somebody go into her apartment — or maybe the one next door. And I can't blame them for not being sure. The hallway's so anonymous. The only descriptions that might help are one of a woman who sounds a lot like Rhonda Stonecipher. But she says she was home all afternoon and Tony Belton says he was with her. I guess they could both be lying."

"She's a type anyway," Shelley said. "Any well-dressed, well-groomed, rich-looking woman of the same age and coloring could be mistaken for her."

"The other description we got of someone who actually might have gone into the apartment sounds quite a lot like your friend LeAnne Doherty," Mel said.

Jane sighed. "I was afraid of that." She and Shelley told him about their odd conversation with LeAnne at the grocery store.

"But she didn't say she'd been there?" Mel asked when they had stopped talking.

"She didn't *say* anything, just asked a lot

of strange questions. Like how well Jane knew you and what you'd told her," Shelley said. "And what you'd found in the apartment."

"It wasn't what she said so much as her manner," Jane added. "She was very nervous. White-knuckled and high-pitched. But Mel, you can't really suspect her."

"Why not? Because you like her?" he asked, taking another cookie.

"No. Because she isn't the least bit canny."

"Jane," he said with impatience, "criminals can be pretty dumb. That's one of the reasons they get caught so often. In fact, lots of times they seem to almost go out of their way to blab about the crime and make themselves look suspicious. A surprising number of them actually make scrapbooks of the clippings about the crime."

"Mel, don't say that. I don't want it to be LeAnne," Jane admitted. "She's a bit dim, but really nice and she's had a hard enough time of it the last few years."

Mel took his empty milk glass to the sink and rinsed it out. "Okay. If it makes you feel better, I'm inclined to doubt she's the perp anyway. At least on the basis of what we know now."

"Which is?"

"The pathology boys say their first impression is that Weyrich died between one and three. The red-haired woman who might have been your friend LeAnne was seen around noon."

"Thank goodness!" Jane said.

"Now, now! I knew you'd do that if I told you," Mel said regretfully. "It doesn't let her off the hook. Not completely. For one thing, she might have come back. For another, the lab people are basing their preliminary findings on body temperature and it's not all that reliable, especially under the circumstances."

"What circumstances?" Shelley asked.

"The apartment was air-conditioned," Mel said. "And it was set as cold as it can be. We have no idea if the murderer turned it down for some reason and the apartment gradually got colder and colder, or whether Weyrich always kept it cold in there. That alone could account for the missing hour. And there's another factor — she had one of those caller identification things on her phone. She got a call at five minutes after noon that she apparently didn't answer because there's a dial tone on her answering machine at the same time. Maybe she saw who was calling and didn't answer. But maybe she was already dead."

"Who was the call from?" Jane asked eagerly.

Mel smiled at her. "A roofing and siding company. Sorry."

"Mel, how are you ever going to figure this out?" Shelley asked. "It seems like such a huge, amorphous wad of information."

"Slowly. Carefully. Bit by tiny bit," he said grimly. "And without any interference from you two if I can manage it."

Jane and Shelley ignored this comment. "Do you think the two incidents are connected?" Shelley asked. "Emma's death and Stonecipher's?"

"Maybe. When two people from one small office die within a couple days of each other, one by murder and one under strange circumstances, that has to be a possibility," he said.

"Isn't there physical evidence from either one?" Jane asked. "Fibers, fingerprints, blood drops, that kind of thing?"

"Tons in Emma's case, ninety-nine percent of which will turn out to be entirely irrelevant," he said. "And the same is true at the deli. But eventually it'll fall together."

Jane gave him A Look. "You're not telling us everything, are you?"

He just smiled back. “Am I supposed to? How’s Mike liking his new truck?” he asked, signifying that police confidences were over.

— 16 —

Shelley called first thing in the morning. "The paper says Stonecipher's funeral is this morning. Are we going?"

"Shelley, you know how I hate funerals. Do we have to?"

"No, but aren't you curious to see how the grieving widow who was about to divorce the late unlamented carries it off? Her wardrobe choice alone ought to be worth the effort."

"You are a callous woman," Jane said.

"So are you, and you know it."

Jane sighed. "What time?"

"Eleven."

Rhonda Stonecipher had split the difference between grief and gaiety. She wore a gray linen suit with a matching hat that even had a suggestion of a veil. "Where did she find that!" Shelley whispered. "That's a great hat!"

But with the gray suit, she wore a gray, white, and fuschia–striped silk blouse with a matching fabric purse and a drapey fuschia scarf affixed with a large silver pin. It was a stunning outfit. She maintained a dignified and aloof manner, sitting at the front of the church with a number of people who were presumably members of her family or that of her late husband. She dabbed her eyes daintily from time to time with an old-fashioned fabric handkerchief with lacy trim.

There was a man who looked like an older version of Robert Stonecipher, who was presumably his brother. A very small woman with sharp, foxy features stood by him. A middle-aged woman who looked a great deal like Rhonda, without the money to dress as well, was in the front pew as well, with a man who looked like he'd rather be almost anywhere else. A woman in her twenties who must have been Rhonda's daughter because she had Rhonda's features, but very fair coloring, stood next to her mother. She was holding a baby.

"Rhonda must be a grandmother," Jane whispered to Shelley. "She sure keeps that quiet."

Jane found herself feeling sorry for Tony Belton. Rhonda had apparently forced him to sit with her and the family, and he looked miserable. Rhonda shared his hymnal, leaning ever so slightly on his arm. The family members on her other side kept shooting him murderous glances. Or perhaps they were aimed at Rhonda and merely ricocheting.

Jane guessed the Stoneciphers weren't regular churchgoers, or perhaps the minister just didn't know them well. It was a generic service, without any reference to the man's life or circumstances surrounding his death.

Tony Belton gave a very short eulogy with the air of a man who had been forced into it, but did a workmanlike job. He concentrated, without being specific, on Stonecipher's civic interests. "His ideas weren't always popular," he admitted, "but he did what he thought he had to for the greater good of the community." As he meandered off into an account of Stonecipher's education, Jane's attention wandered. The church was less than half full, and those attending the service were widely scattered, as people do when they're attending a funeral out of duty, not friendship.

Patsy Mallett had come in her role as business acquaintance. She was sitting alone and looking down intently, as if she had something in her lap she was reading.

As Jane watched, Patsy wet her finger to turn a page.

Grace Axton was there as well. Also alone. She stared straight ahead, absolutely expressionless, her mind probably a thousand miles away.

There was a contingent of men who had to be lawyers judging by their golf tans and expensive summer suits. A few couples who were probably neighbors were sitting here and there, and several small groups of women filled in some of the gaps. Jane vaguely recognized a few of them as what remained of a once-large segment of society known as "clubwomen"— those ladies whose lives revolved around the garden club, beautification projects, and various good works. Jane found herself cynically wondering how many of them had gotten stuck paying for a lunch or dinner or drink for Rhonda.

When the service was done, Jane whispered, "I don't do gravesides."

"Neither do I," Shelley answered. "I'm surprised Grace was here. Who's that woman she's talking to?"

"That's Patsy Mallett. Come meet her."

Jane introduced the two women and left them gingerly assessing each other while she walked out to the parking lot with

Grace Axton. "I was surprised to see you here," she said frankly to Grace.

"I thought since the man actually died in our place, somebody should show up. But it was a mistake. I've never felt like such a hypocrite in my life," Grace replied.

"Is Sarah home from the hospital?" Jane asked. Grace nodded while rummaging in her purse for car keys. "How's she doing?"

"Oh, fine. Fine. I think she'd be better if Conrad would stop protecting her. But it's none of my business. I've got to rush, Jane."

"Sure. I didn't mean to hold you up."

Shelley and Patsy emerged from the church a minute later, talking and nodding. Good, Jane thought. Often people who were a lot alike got along well. Occasionally they took an instant dislike to each other. But it looked as if Shelley and Patsy were hitting it off great. Jane finally pried them apart and drove home. "We're meeting Patsy at two to talk about the high school graduation night plans for next year," Shelley said. "Fascinating woman."

When Jane got home, Todd was sitting at the kitchen table eating a bowl of cereal and fending off the cats, who were sitting on chairs, watching every slurpy bite and hoping for a milk spill. "Mike's been calling and calling, Mom. You're supposed to call him back at the deli."

Alarmed, Jane dialed. Mike answered. "What's wrong?" she asked.

"Calm down, Mom. I just left my billfold at home with my driver's license."

"Oh, is that all! You scared me. Why didn't you just come home and get it?"

"Because there's a cop sitting out front with a speed trap."

"Then don't speed or walk home."

Mike didn't even bother to scoff at the idea of walking. "Mom, you want to talk about what'll happen to your insurance rates if he decides to stop me anyhow and I'm driving without a license?"

"Okay, okay. You're right. Where's the billfold?"

She ventured into his room, trying not to see the piles of dirty laundry, trying not to think how very soon this room would be unoccupied most of the time and dirty laundry would be a welcome sight, and found the billfold just where he said it was. Instead of parking in front, she pulled through the alley and parked next to Mike's truck in the back. He was loading carry-out lunches into the back. She handed over the billfold.

"Thanks, Mom. Listen —" he said,

taking her aside and lowering his voice. "Something weird. I parked here this morning about an hour ago, went inside to help out, and when I came back out, I realized somebody had been in the truck."

"What?"

"They didn't take anything. There's nothing to take. I left my portable CD player at home today. I guess maybe somebody knew I had one and was going to grab it."

"If nothing's missing, how do you know somebody got into the truck?"

"Because the seat was pushed back as far as it can go."

"Good Lord! Do you think someone was trying to steal it?"

"I don't know, but I'm locking it up every time I get out now. And if you park back here again, you should, too."

"Mike, I'd pay somebody to steal the station wagon," she joked.

"Lock it up anyway," he said seriously. "There's lots of kids around here and they were probably just looking over the truck, but still — come inside. Conrad has something he wants you to try. I've got to go. See you later."

Jane did as he suggested, then knocked on the back door to the kitchen. Sarah opened the door. "Oh, Jane. Good. Conrad wants you to try the artichoke dip. It's a new recipe."

"Sarah?" Conrad said, "What are you doing down here? I told you I don't need any help. You should be upstairs resting. Hi, Jane. Come on in."

Grace was cutting up spring onions. "Conrad, she's rested all morning," she said.

"Yes, honey. I need something to do," Sarah said.

"Not until you're back up to speed," he said firmly, giving her a light kiss and a gentle shove toward the stairway.

Sarah went without any more protest, but Jane saw Grace's back stiffen.

Conrad gestured to Jane to sit at the small desk by the phone. He brought over a plate with an assortment of crackers and a little dish of steaming dip. "Careful. It's still hot."

Jane tested the dip. "Wonderful! What's in it?"

"Artichokes, beer, cream cheese, and some seasonings," he said, pleased. "The trick is keeping it from getting too runny. Now here's some from the same batch that's cooled."

"Conrad, I think it's even better warm than hot," Jane decided.

Grace, finished with her job, came and sat down. "That's what I think, too. But Conrad's fretting about keeping it hot."

He shrugged. "Two to one against me. I guess I'm beaten."

"What does Sarah think?" Jane asked.

"Oh, Sarah doesn't like artichokes," he said. "She loved them when we were kids," Grace said with surprise.

"People change," he replied.

Grace started to say something, but, sensing tension, Jane changed the subject. "Mike was sure loaded down with luncheons. It's going well?"

"Wonderfully well. Except for the raccoons," Grace said with a smile. "They dumped all the trash out of the barrels last night. We're going to have to get something with locked lids."

Jane almost mentioned someone getting into Mike's truck, planning to make a joke about raccoons being smart enough to drive, but decided against it. Conrad had enough on his mind without worrying about neighborhood kids prowling around behind the deli.

When Jane returned home, Shelley was wrestling her hose and sprinkler around from the back yard to the front. "Are you trying to make it rain?" Jane asked. "I know where you could get a nice little pamphlet on lawn care."

"If that old bastard tries to give me one of his pamphlets, he'll find it stuck up his nose in seconds," Shelley said, bending down and studying the dial setting on the sprinkler. She adjusted it, went back to the faucet, and turned it on. "Where have you been?"

Jane explained her trip to the deli. "Conrad sent home some dip. Come in and try it while I change my clothes."

When she was comfortably clad in jeans and a T-shirt that said, "World's Greatest Mom," she found Shelley sitting on the sofa, making dainty smacking noises with her eyes closed. "Paprika, I think," she said, analyzing the dip. "I don't suppose he told you what the seasonings were."

"I didn't ask. Shelley, it's a little tense there."

"What do you mean?"

Shelley picked up the little Styrofoam carton of dip and followed Jane to the kitchen, where Jane poured them both a glass of iced tea, then nipped out the back door to pluck some mint leaves to put in it.

"It's like Conrad and Grace are having a tug of war with Sarah," Jane said. "They both adore her and want what's best, but they seem to have different ideas of what that is. Conrad treats her like a piece of porcelain that has to be protected from everything — including herself. Grace seems to be more down-to-earth and practical, wanting to let Sarah take care of herself. At least a little bit."

"That's too bad," Shelley said. "I'm on Grace's side, but I can see how it's awkward. Conrad is her husband, after all, and knows her best. Even Grace admitted that Sarah's a different person whom she hardly knows anymore. Sarah might be a whole lot more fragile than Grace realizes."

"True. And I imagine Grace has thought of that, but it's awkward for her. It's always awkward being a fifth wheel anyway."

Shelley waited for Jane to go on, and when she didn't, said, "There's something else on your mind, too, isn't there?"

"That obvious? Okay, this makes me feel like a real traitor, but I've been wondering about Grace. That nasty divorce of hers — how long ago was it?"

"I don't know. Years and years, I imagine."

"Before Stonecipher moved here?"

Shelley was silent for a few minutes. "I see what you mean. She might have been another client like LeAnne. I'll have to think about this. I believe it was much longer ago than that, but then I don't really know when Stonecipher first turned up."

"How can we find out?" Jane asked.

"Didn't you say Patsy Mallett was an old friend of Grace's? She'd know who handled her divorce."

"You're not thinking of just asking her outright, are you? She'd see through what you were getting at in a minute. Patsy's no dummy."

"Jane! Don't you think I can be subtle?" Shelley said with a grin.

"I merely think you've met your match in Patsy. But I look forward to watching — at a safe distance."

– 17 –

Jane was thrilled to discover that Patsy Mallett lived in the messiest house in the world. It wasn't dirty though. Clean windows, floors, curtains, no used dishes sitting out on the sink. But for sheer numbers of "things" out and about, Patsy took the prize. There were piles of books and papers everywhere. Tidy piles, but a lot of them. Plastic bags bulged with needlework, model airplanes, electronic kits. There were a dozen different rosters on the telephone table, half a dozen notepads, children's artwork, some yellowed and curling, adorned the front of the refrigerators and the walls. A stack of recipe books was feathered with notes and file cards sticking out every which way.

Patsy ushered Jane and Shelley into a huge family room with a picnic-sized table in the middle, nearly covered with other projects in various stages of completion. A clay model, sketchpads, some colored chalk, and poster-board took up most of the surface. Three sides of the rooms were windows and had glass shelving with plants everywhere. One whole large window had spectacular African violets. Another was cacti and succulents. There were bonsai trees, radishes growing in cut-down milk cartons, and something that looked like an experiment in hydroponics. A sweet-potato vine started near the kitchen door and worked its way entirely around the room.

They had to make their way around a sewing table, spinning wheel, and loom to get to the table, where Patsy was hastily clearing a spot for them to sit without their elbows in a project. It was a fascinating house reflecting an enormous variety of interests and skills.

"I know it's a mess, but it's my house," Patsy said with a laugh. "When I turned fifty, I decided I was entitled to live any way I wanted without apology. It was tremendously liberating. My late mother-in-law used to give me a cleaning service every year for my birthday and they always quit within the month because they couldn't stand all the stuff. There, I think that will give us a little space. Jane, you can sit over here, just watch where you step."

Alarmed for a second, Jane glanced down. Pushed up against the wall by the chair was a cardboard box containing a fluffy towel, a big tawny cat, and four of the cutest kittens Jane had ever seen. "Oh, how pretty they are!" she said, squatting on the floor. "Will the mother let me touch them?"

"Only if you give her a good petting first," Patsy said. "They're Abyssinians. Aren't they lush little guys?"

Jane sat down cross-legged on the floor and played with the kittens while Shelley and Patsy started going over the basic outline of the high school graduation night party. Patsy had charts showing who reported to whom, a day-by-day plan for the year that put the most elaborate "Plan Your Wedding" chart to shame. She had notebooks for each committee and subcommittee, which gave the entire history of their work from inception, all suppliers they'd ever used with assessments of each, and annual budgets balanced down to the last penny. There were scrapbooks that captured each graduation party in pictures, boxes of ribbons and buttons that identified the workers, and small plastic containers of attractive tiny lapel pins to reward the workers. Patsy had had her collection of pins made into charms on a bracelet, which she showed them with well-deserved pride.

Jane was far more interested in the kittens, who were now climbing around on her, but got the impression from what she overheard of the conversation between the other two women that Patsy thought all this organization was not only easy but fun. And Shelley agreed. The strongest of the kittens had climbed up the front of Jane's T-shirt to her shoulder, and after studying her ear with great concentration, licked her earlobe with its tiny emery-board tongue. Jane's heart turned into marshmallow goo.

By the time the kittens started to tire, nearly an hour had passed. Shelley and Patsy were winding up their overview of the graduation night party's history and methods. Jane tucked the exhausted kittens into the box where the mother cat had been calmly sleeping, and joined Shelley at the table. Patsy was putting away notebooks. "What did I miss?" Jane asked with a guilty grin.

"I signed you up for six committees," Shelley said. "You don't need a personal life, do you?"

"You've been talking to my kids if you think that."

"Actually, Patsy thinks I might be good

as junior co-chairman of the food committee and you've agreed to assist me," Shelley said. "You *do* agree?"

"I wouldn't think of disagreeing with the two of you. Patsy, there are people like you and Shelley who like running things, and people like me who will do anything Shelley tells me to —"

"Not quite anything," Shelley murmured. "I told you a white winter coat was a waste of money."

"— but," Jane continued, "there are a lot of people who can't stand being told what to do by anybody. How on earth do you manage? Everybody seems to come out of this still liking you."

"Kindness," Patsy answered. "Deadly kindness. There are plenty of people who don't like me, but since I'm so terribly, *terribly* nice to them, they can't quite figure out why and are embarrassed to say so. Being kind to someone puts them in your power."

"Are you being kind to us?" Jane asked.

Patsy laughed. "I hope so, but it's because I like you two so much. How about some cookies and coffee?"

Jane glanced around the busy room. "If you're a good cook, too, I might have to kill you."

Patsy laughed heartily. "Don't worry. My family has nearly banned me from the kitchen. My kids are all good cooks out of self-defense. They'd have starved otherwise. I've mastered egg salad sandwiches and that's about it. But my oldest daughter came by last night and made the cookies. Stay where you are."

She bustled off to the kitchen while Shelley studied the one notebook that was left on the table. As Jane watched her, Shelley suddenly did something very odd. Her eyes widened, she looked down and said, in the sappiest voice Jane had ever heard, "Ooooh, my."

Jane stood up and leaned over the table to look. The mother cat had deposited a sleeping, milk-sated kitten in Shelley's lap.

Shelley, who despised cats, looked up at Jane and said in a tiny voice, "That's so sweet I think I'm going to cry." She gathered the kitten up tenderly and held its little soft body to her face. "What a baby!"

Patsy came back in with a tray. "She wants you to have that one," she said.

"No, no. I hate cats," Shelley said. She had her eyes closed and the kitten against her cheek.

"They'll be ready for new homes in about two more weeks," Patsy said as she poured coffee. "Jane, you need one, too."

Jane shook her head regretfully. "I have two cats already who would probably consider these little guys chipmunks. And my dog would either be afraid of them or think they were snacks. These cookies are wonderful! And the coffee is — well, *hot*."

Patsy didn't take offense. "Best I can do. Would you prefer tea? I boil water well and you could drop the tea bag into the cup yourself."

The sludgy coffee was removed, Shelley reluctantly put the kitten back in its box, and the three women applied themselves to cookies and Earl Grey tea. "Strangely impersonal funeral this morning, wasn't it?" Patsy said. "I felt sorry for Tony Belton."

"Me, too," Jane said. "He didn't seem pleased at the way Rhonda latched on to him. What do you suppose the nature of their relationship really is?"

"I don't know. I've only seen Tony at the office when I went in to pick up paperwork," Patsy said. "I've always thought he was a nice young man. I wonder what Rhonda has in store for him."

"What do you mean?" Shelley asked.

"Just that I assume her interest in him is self-interest, because she's that kind of person. He's handsome, young, and apparently pretty pliable judging from the fact that he sat up front with the family even though he *and* they were obviously unhappy about it," Patsy said. "But does she plan to marry him or does she think she can profit from him financially?"

"How would she do that?" Jane asked.

"I'm not sure, but Rhonda never lets a penny go without making it scream for mercy. Depending on what kind of partnership agreement Stonecipher and Tony had, she might stand to profit from stringing him along."

"Might they both have profited from her husband's death?" Jane asked.

Patsy shrugged. "I guess it's possible. But I only handled the client billing. How the money was distributed once it came in is anybody's guess."

"But Emma would have known," Jane said.

"Are you thinking they conspired to bump her off?" Patsy asked bluntly.

"Not thinking, exactly, just wondering. After all, somebody did kill her."

"Isn't that odd?" Patsy said. "If you divide people into potential victims and potential perpetrators, I'd have put her firmly on the perpetrator side. I didn't have many dealings with her, but I had the feeling she had a strong instinct for the main chance."

"But she was victimized by Stonecipher, apparently, and for a long time," Shelley said.

"Yes, but that was sex," Patsy said. "Whole different category. How are the police getting along with their investigation of her death? The article in the paper this morning was awfully vague."

"Badly," Jane said. "There were two other things going on at the apartment building at the same time. A party and a garage sale. Apparently half the town was in and out all afternoon. They need someone like you to organize all the information," she added with a smile.

"I hear she was blackmailing people," Patsy said.

"Where did you hear that?" Jane said, surprised.

"Oh, here and there," Patsy said with a smile. "I have my sources. Actually, the police must have been asking people about some kind of file folders. File folders contain information and information is a saleable commodity. It doesn't take a rocket scientist to make the connection."

Shelley had been quiet. Now she said, "I was surprised to see Grace Axton at the funeral this morning. You'd think as much grief as Stonecipher had given them, she'd have just been glad he was gone."

"Grace feels strongly about appearances and manners," Patsy said. "Some Puritan strain in her. Most of us would have thought we should show up and then thought up excuses not to. But Grace doesn't give herself excuses. She's a tough lady. Tougher with herself than anyone else. At least since her divorce, which was about the same time we met in an accounting class. She had to be strong to get out of that marriage in the first place, and then make a life and profession for herself. I really admire her."

"How long ago was the divorce?" Shelley asked.

"Oh, a good ten years ago, I think. Maybe only eight or nine. And she was just starting out with her accounting business when Sarah went to pieces. She had to drop everything. Grace's ex-husband had disappeared and wasn't making the house payments like the settlement ordered. Grace gave up the house, her fledgling business, and everything to go to her sister. That's how she ended up living with her grandmother when it was all over. But I never once heard her complain."

"Poor Grace. And poor Sarah," Jane

said. "I can't imagine having only the one child and never even getting to take it home."

Patsy looked at her curiously. "What do you mean, never take it home?"

"Wasn't it born with brain damage? That's what Grace said."

Patsy shook her head. "I think you misunderstood. The baby was born normal. He was a year old when he died."

"Oh. I guess I did."

"I misunderstood, too," Shelley added. "But now that I think about it, Grace just said they had a child who was severely brain damaged. She didn't say it was born that way. What happened to the child?"

"It drowned in the bathtub," Patsy said. "Well, didn't quite drown. Sarah had forgotten and left something on the stove, smelled it burning, and dashed to turn off the burner. She was only gone a few seconds, but it was long enough. The paramedics did their job too well. It would have been better if they hadn't revived — oh, well. Not for me to say, I guess. Anyway, the baby never regained consciousness, was on life support. It must have been horrible. About the only thing in its little brain that didn't die was whatever triggered convulsions."

Jane was appalled. "Oh, that's so much worse than I imagined. And it goes a long way toward explaining why Sarah is still unbalanced. It wasn't just fate, it was her fault. How unutterably awful."

"I'm sorry. I guess I shouldn't have told you," Patsy said. "It's horrible even knowing, but it does explain Sarah's condition. And Grace's concern."

Shelley stood up and came around to the cat's box. "I need to cuddle a kitten," she said.

"We all need to," Patsy said with a smile. "Shelley, you know you've fallen in love with them. Why don't you just admit it to yourself?"

"No way," Shelley said, stroking the mother cat. "I don't like cats. Never have. What's her name?"

"Abby," Patsy said. "Not very original."

"Don't feel bad. Shelley's got a French poodle named Frenchie," Jane said. "She may be my best friend, but I have to say she's not good at names. I've always been sort of amazed that she didn't name her children Boy and Girl."

— 18 —

"You know you're going to cave in," Jane said as they drove home.

"No, I'm not," Shelley said. "Those kittens just cast a temporary spell over me. Now that I'm away from them, I'll get over it in no time."

But she still had a dreamy, goofy look on her face.

Jane glanced at her watch. "There's supposed to be a soccer practice at four. I imagine it's canceled."

"Why?"

"Won't Tony Belton still be tied up with funeral stuff? You don't suppose Rhonda will let go of him so he can coach a bunch of little boys," Jane said.

They pulled into Jane's driveway. Shelley said, "There's a calling committee. If it's been canceled somebody will have told us."

But neither of them had a message on her answering machine. And since it was beginning to cloud up, they decided to drive the boys to the practice later and stick around to remove them if it rained. Jane had an hour to kill, looked around the kitchen — which appeared to have been the site of a food explosion — and decided it could wait to be cleaned up. She went to the basement with the intention of getting a little writing done and ended up playing solitaire on the computer while her mind churned over Emma's death.

By the time Shelley knocked on the door upstairs, Jane had done nothing but further confuse and frustrate herself. They rounded up their boys and Suzie Williams's son and went to pick up the other two in their car pool and delivered them to the soccer field behind the high school. Summer vacation was still new enough that the boys were hyper and the trip seemed much longer than it really was. Tony Belton was already out on the field, demonstrating various techniques to the early birds.

"I'm surprised he doesn't have a glamorous middle-aged widow still hanging on his arm," Shelley said.

"If you look closely, though, you can see the talon marks," Jane said.

A few other mothers and one father were sitting in the bleachers, but Shelley and

Jane didn't know any of them well enough to feel obligated to sit with them. Instead, they settled by a pile of paperwork and equipment in the center front that presumably belonged to Tony Belton. Shelley was fidgety.

"What's on your mind?" Jane finally asked.

Shelley thought for a minute and said, "Well, I'm hardly even willing to consider it, much less talk about it, but has it occurred to you that Patsy Mallett is a very strong, determined woman and —"

"And a very likeable one," Jane said, nodding.

"Yes, that's why I'm reluctant to even say this, but she did know both Stonecipher and Emma."

"Right. I have to admit I thought about that, too. But while she knows a little about them, what could Emma have known about her? That seems to be the key here."

"Something dreadful about the bookkeeping she does?" Shelley suggested.

"Like fudging some extra profit out for herself? I guess it's possible in theory," Jane said. "But you'd have to put a cattle prod to the small of my back to make me believe it. If nothing else, there's the practical consideration: if you were going to cheat somebody, would you pick a particularly bad-natured attorney?"

"Not unless you were sure you could get away with it and were cheating everybody. I don't believe she's capable of it either, but I had to say it, just to get it out of my head. It makes me feel slimy to even think about it."

"That's the tough thing about this," Jane said. "There's nobody but maybe Rhonda that I'd really like to pin this on. And she's not even a good villain, just an annoying woman."

"Speaking of annoying women —" Shelley said, gesturing toward a newcomer who was dragging coolers and cardboard boxes out of a station wagon. The team's mothers took turns bringing snacks for the boys to indulge in after the practice. Jane, Shelley, and several others had objected repeatedly and almost violently to this tradition on the grounds that the boys went from soccer practice straight home to dinners they didn't want to eat because they were full of snacks. But the tradition persisted. Most of the mothers at least attempted to bring something halfway healthy, but one — the one now approaching the field — brought the most appetite-repressing things she could find. Sodas instead of juice, Twinkies and chocolate-chip cookies instead of granola bars, and far too much of everything. Nobody could figure out whether she did it to be hateful, or just had no common sense.

"I think she means it well," Jane said, trying to be generous. "She likes that stuff, her tubby little boy obviously loves it, and for that matter, so do the rest of the boys. Her kid probably goes home and tucks away all his dinner, and she wonders why the rest of us have such picky eaters."

When the practice was over and the boys fell on the snacks like a pack of hyenas, Tony Belton approached the bleachers. He greeted them by name and sat down to glance through the notebooks containing his team roster and make notes.

"We were a bit surprised to see you here," Shelley said. "We thought with the funeral just this morning . . ." She let the rest of the sentence hanging for him to pick up.

He did so. "Rhon— Mrs. Stonecipher didn't really need me at the house. She's got a lot of family there. A *lot* of family," he added with a smile.

"Still, I'm sure it's been a great boon to her to have your support," Shelley said.

"I hope so. Robert and I didn't always get along as well as we might, but I owed him a lot, and if I can help his wife get through a bad time, I'm happy to do it."

Jane and Shelley exchanged a quick look. Jane made a little go-ahead gesture.

"I guess he was hard to get along with," Shelley prodded.

Tony Belton closed his notebook. "Anybody with such strong opinions sometimes rubs people the wrong way. But as a mentor, he was tops. He really knew the law inside and out. I think I learned as much from him in four years as I did in law school."

"Is that when you joined his firm? Is it a firm when it's just one person?" Jane asked.

Tony smiled. "I'd have to research that. Actually, Robert and I both turned up here at the same time and a mutual acquaintance introduced us. I'd grown up here, then practiced in Connecticut for years. When I got divorced, I came back so that when I have my son here and have to work, he could be with my parents instead of a babysitter."

"What a good idea," Jane said.

"It's worked out pretty well. My folks spoil him rotten. But then, so do I."

"How old is your son?"

"The same age as your boys. He'll be here for the summer next week and be on the team. His school isn't out yet."

Shelley politely asked him about his son and they got a run-down on what a great kid he was. Tony was a besotted father. Finally Jane dragged the topic back. "So Mr. Stonecipher came here at the same time?"

"Right. He'd had a successful practice, but the pressure had gotten too much, so he and his wife came back here — she's from Chicago originally — to retire. But a man of his energy couldn't really retire so early and he was just starting up a new practice when I met him."

"And where does Emma Weyrich come into this?" Shelley asked bluntly.

If the question made him wary, he didn't show it. "She'd worked with him out West, and he invited her here when he started getting things lined up."

"Was she that good at whatever she did?"

"Sure, Robert wouldn't bother with anybody who wasn't good. Well, that sounds big-headed of me —"

"Not at all," Shelley said. "But I get the feeling you didn't like her much."

That did make him pause carefully. Jane guessed that he wasn't normally given to talking about himself so much, but had been inundated with Rhonda's concerns for the last couple days and perhaps appreciated somebody asking about him for a change.

"I didn't dislike her," he said, sounding more like a lawyer than a soccer coach.

"But you weren't entirely thrilled to work with her?" Shelley prodded.

"I didn't 'work with her' much. She worked with Robert, not me. Research, mainly. And some routine minor filings. Property settlements, that sort of thing."

"You knew they were having an affair?" Jane asked.

He looked surprised. Not at the information but at Jane's knowing it. "It was none of my business."

"Then what — ?"

"Look, I don't know why this interests you, but Emma was an advice giver. One of those people who's always volunteering what you ought to be doing about things, whether you wanted her opinion or not. I didn't like it. She had all kinds of half-assed opinions on how I should be raising my son. Coming from a woman who didn't have children and hadn't been asked, it was really irritating. That's all."

He was obviously getting irritated with their questions as well. It was time for some repair work.

"No!" Jane exclaimed. "Why, how outrageous. But there are a lot of people like that. In fact, people without kids often think they know more about raising them than the parents like us who are in the trenches."

This mollified him a bit. "Yeah, there's a big difference between theory and reality. She had a loony idea about year-round school and how I should make him take summer classes when he visited with me. She was always harping on it. Thought it would make for great 'bonding' if I spent every night all summer helping him with homework. I don't think she was ever a kid herself," he added sourly.

"But why would somebody kill her?" Jane asked as if pondering the question for the first time.

He shrugged. "You've got me there." He didn't seem particularly curious.

"There's a rumor going around that she was blackmailing people," Shelley said.

"Blackmailing? Really?" He seemed genuinely surprised. "What would she know about anybody? Oh — !" He stopped speaking, his mouth open.

"What?" Jane asked.

He was glaring out across the now empty field and talking to himself more than to them. "The police asked me about some files in Robert's office — private files, they said. Oh, shit! You don't think —"

Suddenly he got a grip on himself. "Sorry. Excuse my language. God, this is awful!" He started gathering up equipment. "Boys, finish up quickly now. It's time to go," he barked.

Jane decided, since he was unravelling, she'd push him just a little further. "I guess you and Rhonda will be getting married when this is all settled."

"What!" It was a yelp.

"Aren't you? Oh, I'm sorry. But we heard that's why she was divorcing her husband."

"She's telling people that?" he asked, dropping his notebook and pencil. "No, no. She wouldn't. No. Mrs. Stonecipher and I are just friends. Really. Boys! Are you ready? Are your rides all here?"

He scrabbled for his notebook and went tearing off to hustle them along.

"Jeez, Jane!" Shelley said, laughing. "What a reaction. You scared him half to death."

"I think it's Rhonda who's scaring him," Jane said.

Shelley watched as Tony Belton started herding the boys toward the waiting cars. "I don't think any of that was an act, do you? I think the blackmailing news was really a kidney punch."

"Mel's going to have a fit if it gets back to him that I talked about it. But if Patsy Mallett's figured it out, I imagine a lot of people have. Wonder why Tony didn't?"

"When's he had time to figure anything out?" Shelley said. "Rhonda's been leading him around by the nose, making him fetch and carry and write eulogies and call relatives. He can't be too stupid to have seen what the police were getting at if he'd had time to consider about it. From his viewpoint, it must be pretty devastating. Whatever his role is in what remains of the firm, think how bad it'll look when it's public knowledge that Stonecipher and Weyrich were keeping blackmail files."

"Wow! I hadn't thought about that!" Jane said.

"But Tony is," Shelley said. "Poor guy. And then you hit him with that marrying Rhonda thing. That was a master stroke, Jane."

"Rhonda sure wouldn't have been flattered at the way he reacted."

They headed toward the car, just as they heard the first roll of thunder.

Shelley pointed at the sky. "Please note! My lawn watering worked."

— 19 —

It was pouring down rain by the time they got home. They'd dropped off the other boys in the car pool and their own two had hopped out. As she got out, Shelley said, "Being in a closed car with a bunch of sweaty twelve-year-old boys is not one of life's dreams. In fact, we may have just had a glimpse of what hell really is like."

Jane went inside and contemplated the contents of the refrigerator. It was a rare treat to have a range of choices. Of course anything she made would seem ordinary after she'd eaten so much of Conrad's marvelous cooking lately. The rain had been swept in by surprisingly cold air, and Jane thought a stew might be nice, but it was too late to start one. She rejected chili because it wasn't cold *enough* outside for that and settled on hamburgers, macaroni and cheese, corn, and a salad. Good, plain food.

Katie came into the kitchen and offered to help. Jane tried to hide her astonishment. She put the macaroni and cheese into the oven, started making the hamburger patties, and set Katie to work on the salad.

"That's not veal, is it?" Katie asked suspiciously.

"Veal? Of course not."

"Because I saw a program on television about veal and the way the poor little calves are kept in these tiny pens —"

"Katie, please. I know. And I don't want to hear about it. I can't afford veal anyway so it will never be a political issue around here."

"But not buying it because you can't afford it isn't the same as not buying it because it's immoral," Katie said.

"Comes to the same thing," Jane said, putting plastic wrap over the plate of hamburgers and checking on the macaroni.

"Mom, don't you care about stuff like that?"

This sort of question was normally rhetorical and belligerent, but this time Katie seemed to be asking it sincerely. "Katie, there's so much in the world that a person could be upset about that you could be miserable every minute of the day. Come sit down. The salad looks good."

They sat at the kitchen table. "It's so

hard to be your age," Jane said.

"Yeah, you're telling me!" Katie said.

"You're just starting to really notice the world around you — in an adult way," Jane went on. "And there's a lot wrong with it. But there's a lot right with it, too. A lot of good things."

Katie nodded. "Like those little kids at the Vacation Bible School. Mom, they're so cute."

"You're liking this job, then?"

"Sure. It's fun. Too bad they're not paying me better," she said, descending from her high moral plateau to the purely practical.

Jane bit back the response that she and Katie were both lucky Katie had any kind of summer job, otherwise they'd be in each other's hair all the time. As it was, they still had all of August to drive each other crazy since the bible school only ran through June and July.

"So, why don't you care about the cute little calves?" Katie asked, unwilling to let the subject go.

"I do care, but there are things I care about a lot more. You and Mike and Todd being at the top of the list and taking up a lot of space. And then I pick and choose pretty carefully what else goes on my particular list. I drive my group of blind kids to their school once a week during the year because the school can't afford bus service and that's a little way I can help. I helped at the graduation night party, which I think is worthwhile. I work on fundraising things for good causes like —"

"But Mom, those are nice things, but they're so — so small. I'm talking about big problems. Like the environment and peace and stuff like that."

"I know. But since I haven't got the slightest idea how to ensure world peace and nobody would have any reason to listen to me even if I thought I knew, I do what I can."

"Well, I want to do something important!" Katie said.

"I hope you do. I think you will someday. And if you want my advice, pick *one* thing that you think is most important. Do you know about the man who had a heart attack at the deli the day it opened?"

"Uh-huh. Gross! Dying there in the middle of all that food!"

"The point is, he was one of those people who couldn't pick a cause and stick to it. He had a new cause every couple weeks. And he didn't get very far with any of them because he'd made so many people mad with the ones that went before. Someday," she added with a grin, "when you're old enough to appreciate it, I'll introduce you to Patsy Mallett. You could probably take over the world with her philosophy. But I don't think you're cynical enough to appreciate it yet."

Jane got up to check on the progress of dinner, and Katie started setting the table.

Be still my heart, Jane said silently. For the first time in years she and her daughter had gotten through a serious discussion, albeit a short theoretical one, without Katie stomping off and slamming doors. There was hope for them.

After dinner, Jane went into the living room and moved an easy chair where she could sit and just look at the rain soaking the back yard. Her floundering vegetable garden would be happy even if the petunias already had their faces down in the mud. Max and Meow came in and got into tidy watchful positions in front of the window, glaring at the rain as if it were a personal affront.

Jane found herself thinking back to what she'd said to Katie about Stonecipher and his causes. In retrospect, she decided she'd been wrong. It wasn't merely that he went from one cause to another, it was that all of them were essentially adversarial to someone else with a lot at stake. Unlike Jane's own driving of the blind children or working at the graduation night party or helping raise funds to replace dangerously out-of-date playground equipment at the park — in which there were no "enemies"— Stonecipher's causes always pitted him against someone else: property owners, individual businesses, and people's personal freedoms.

His causes also made him highly visible. Which, the more Jane thought about it, could have been the basic motivation. Maybe his real desire was simply to show off and garner lots of attention. Of course, Jane's view of him now was highly colored by knowing about his nasty secret file cabinet. She simply couldn't believe that somebody who was basically immoral could sincerely espouse moral causes.

Trying to be fair, if only in her own mind, Jane reminded herself that there was no proof that Stonecipher had ever made use of the files. But even if he hadn't used them yet, why would a person keep such things if he didn't intend to gain from them eventually?

Emma certainly hadn't hesitated once Stonecipher was dead. Maybe Stonecipher kept the files just because he liked "having things" on people. Like the miser counting his coins. But Emma had almost instantly seen a way to invest those coins and turn them into more capital. But just how successful could that have been? If Jane's own file was an example, Emma's ploy would have failed. Stonecipher had speculated that the Jeffry pharmacies might be involved in some sort of fraud, but he'd been wrong, so there was no blackmail potential in it.

If Emma hadn't died and Jane had met with her, Jane would have been offended, but definitely wouldn't have parted with a penny. But she certainly hated having a file of any sort being batted around as part of a murder investigation. Maybe Emma had better (or worse, depending on your viewpoint) things about the other people she'd intended to get her hooks into. That might have accounted for why she was content to see Jane late in the day.

The phone rang. "What are you doing?" Shelley asked.

"Looking at the rain. Thinking about things I should be doing and don't want to."

"Paul's taken the kids to the movies and I'm rattling around by myself. Want some company?"

She arrived a few minutes later with a plate full of iced sugar cookies. "I'm here in self-defense," she said. "I'd have eaten them all by myself if I'd stayed home."

Mike came in as they were settling down with coffee and cookies and helped get rid of quite a few of them. He went upstairs, taking a couple more to Katie and Todd. "See how easy it was to solve that problem?" Jane asked, looking at the decimated plate.

"Not really," Shelley said. "There are another two dozen at home. I got carried away and tripled the recipe. Speaking of problems, I've been thinking about Emma. And money."

"Oh?"

"We've been obsessing on the blackmail thing. Assuming that if she was blackmailing someone, that was why she was killed."

"Sounds like a good assumption to me," Jane said.

"It is. But it's not necessarily the only possible reason. Look at how many people had an interest in the money the law firm generated. Stonecipher, his wife, his partner, his assistant. Even Patsy is involved in a peripheral way since she handled the billing. Now two of those people are dead. One from natural causes but under very odd circumstances, and one was murdered."

"Yes," Jane said, "but what does this lead to?"

"I'm not sure. I'm just thinking out loud. The talk is that the Stoneciphers paid too much for their house. You can tell to look at it that they invested a fortune into it. And now it looks like Rhonda is trying to get her hooks into Tony Belton — the remaining lawyer in the firm — and he's resisting. So, couldn't there be a big money problem? Suppose, for example, that the firm was bringing in huge amounts, but Tony Belton was really generating all the business instead of Robert. If Rhonda was already sick and tired of her husband, it might account for her filing for divorce, then trying to grab on to Tony."

"Right. But what would any of this have to do with Emma?"

"I'm not sure, except that she'd apparently been Stonecipher's mistress for years. She must have had dirt on Rhonda. And she would have been bright enough to know who was the real source of the firm's income. Maybe she wanted to latch on to Tony, too. Couldn't Rhonda have been afraid of Emma wrecking her plans?"

"So Rhonda killed her to get rid of the competition?" Jane asked.

"It's possible, isn't it?" Shelley took a cookie and munched for a moment before adding, "Unlikely. But possible."

"I'd vote for unlikely, if not downright impossible. Conning people out of a few lunches is a long way from being greedy enough to actually kill a rival for the sake of money. If all Rhonda wanted was a richer husband, there are a fair number of available older men with money."

"But they all want young bimbos, Jane. It's a tough marriage market for middle-aged women, no matter how well-preserved they may be. Oh, well. Maybe I'm just obsessing on money because I had to pay the quarterly taxes today."

"Shelley, you know I'm not one to discount money as a good motive for practically anything, but I just don't see the tie-in. I wish I could. I know Mel doesn't believe I had anything to do with this, but I absolutely *hate* the fact that my name and private business is in a file folder in a police evidence room, or safe, or whatever. If this case isn't solved, every few months or years, somebody will go back over all the available evidence, come around asking questions again, and I'll never hear the end of it."

Shelley nodded. "True enough. If the murder had something to do with money, Patsy Mallett would be the one who knew the most about the firm's income."

"And she'd never tell us," Jane said. "I have the feeling she probably has unbendable rules about discussing her clients' business."

"But she'd tell the police," Shelley said.

Mike came through the room again, having showered and changed his clothes. "I'm off, Mom," he said, eyeing the last cookie.

"Go ahead and take it," Shelley said. "There are more."

"Where are you going?" Jane asked.

"Wherever the four winds take me," he said, striking a pose.

"Oh, good answer!" Jane said with a laugh. "A lot more poetic than some others I've heard over the years. Don't be late," she added automatically.

"I don't have to work tomorrow so it doesn't matter," Mike said. "Scott's starting deliveries at the deli tomorrow and I get the day off because I worked Saturday."

"Oh, fair enough. Is that the doorbell?"

"It's probably Scott," Mike said, but a moment later Mel VanDyne came into the living room.

"Sorry to drop in without warning," he said, "but I've been trying to call you for half an hour. If you don't get your daughter her own phone line, I'm going to."

Shelley ran home to restock the cookie supply while Jane made a fresh pot of coffee. When they were all comfortably re-settled in the living room, Jane said, "Mel, did you talk to LeAnne Doherty about Emma?"

"Oh, yes. And before I was halfway through my first question, she confessed."

— 20 —

"LeAnne confessed!" Shelley and Jane yelped in unison.

"Hold it! You didn't let me finish," Mel said, alarmed.

"Either she confessed or she didn't," Jane replied. "You said she did."

"Not to murder. To being at Emma's apartment. She was, as you said, a bundle of nerves. She says Emma called her Friday night, told her she was to come by at noon Saturday. Emma told her she had some confidential information that your friend LeAnne might be happier if other people didn't know about. So she went."

"And?"

"And they argued. Mrs. Doherty cried. In the end, Weyrich misjudged badly and demanded so much money that there was simply no way the Dohertys could have paid it even if they wanted to."

"I don't imagine you're going to tell us what the blackmail threat was?" Jane said.

"You're right, I'm not. It wasn't anything

illegal, just embarrassing. Anyway, Mrs. Doherty says she realized the situation was beyond her control, that they'd already weathered a lot of grief and would just have to get through some more if Emma shot off her mouth. Mrs. Doherty claims she told Weyrich to go to hell and left."

"I'll bet she felt relieved," Jane said.

Mel looked at her strangely. "That's exactly what she said. How did you know?"

Jane shrugged. "There's a sort of euphoria when you burn your bridges. Or just accept that things are as they are, can't be changed, and aren't worth thinking about anymore. Even if you don't like the decision you have to make, it feels good to make it and have it over with. Don't you think?"

Mel nodded. "I never looked at it that way, but I guess you're right."

Shelley spoke up. "But that all changed when she found out Emma had been killed and someone might have seen her at the apartment."

"Right," Mel said. "I think if I hadn't gone to interview her, she'd have turned herself in pretty soon. She was really in a state and so was her husband."

"You believe her?" Jane asked.

He cocked an eyebrow. "Provisionally. Somewhat. We'll see."

"Three qualifiers. Not good," Jane said with a smile.

"She *is* the last person who admits to having seen the victim alive. She could be an awfully good actress."

"But she wouldn't have bothered to try an act on me," Jane said.

"Sure she would," Mel said. "For practice, if nothing else. And remember, you told me she was asking you about me and about the investigation. She must have known you'd tell me about it."

"You didn't say that's why —"

"No," Mel said. "I told her someone leaving the retirement party had described seeing a woman who looked like her go into Weyrich's apartment. I hadn't even gotten the words out when she went to pieces and spilled the whole story."

"If you believed her, where would that leave you?" Shelley asked. "Have you learned anything else?"

"As a matter of fact, we have. But it's not much help yet," Mel said. "One of Emma's neighbors saw her come out of her apartment Friday night pretty late. Around eleven. In her jogging gear, but carrying something that jingled on one hand — they thought it was a set of car keys — and a file folder in the other. Or several file folders."

"Friday night," Jane said. "The night of the high school graduation and party. That sounds like she made at least one house call with her little scheme."

"It sure does," Shelley said, "but why a jogging outfit?"

"Maybe she was doing two entirely different things," Jane said. "Dropping in on someone for a spot of blackmail and then going jogging. Don't a lot of people go somewhere to jog instead of just trotting around their own block? I'm always seeing people at that track that runs around the perimeter of the park who don't live adjacent to it."

"Or maybe she was doing two errands at the same time," Shelley said.

"What do you mean?"

"Maybe she was meeting another jogger," Shelley went on. "Either someone she regularly saw wherever she jogged. Or somebody she told to meet her there."

"Why would she risk being overheard?" Jane asked.

"I don't know," Shelley said. "Maybe it was someone she was at least slightly afraid to be alone with. Someone who might have agreed to her demands and then came back Saturday afternoon and killed her."

Jane shivered.

"Where were the suspects on Friday night, Mel?" Shelley asked. "Or have you had time to find out yet?"

Mel glared at her. "Suspects?" he asked, a slightly shrill note in his voice. "Just which suspects are those? Depending on how you look at it, I have either no suspects or a whole city full of them."

"Oh, right," Shelley said. "All the people with files that are missing."

"Right," Mel agreed grimly. "The only suspects as such are Jane, who isn't one really because her file was the one left behind, and she was with me Friday night, and LeAnne Doherty. She, by the way, was at a family party and claims at least fourteen relatives will swear that neither she nor her husband ever left the house Friday night. On top of which, there's absolutely no reason to think whoever Weyrich might have met Friday night is the same person who killed her. In fact, there's only one person that I know of so far in this whole mess who absolutely couldn't have killed Emma Weyrich."

"Who's that?" Jane asked.

"Sarah Baker."

"Sarah?" Shelley exclaimed. "Why would Sarah want to kill anyone?"

"I didn't say she had any reason to —"

"Mel, don't grit your teeth that way," Jane said. "Have another cookie."

"Sorry. I only meant that, of all the people at the deli opening and those who were known to have had dealings with Robert Stonecipher — which is the best I can do in the way of a suspect list — Sarah Baker is the only one with an unbreakable alibi."

"Because she was in the hospital, right?" Jane said. "And she couldn't have sneaked out."

"It's a measure of my desperation that I even checked on that," Mel admitted. "No, she was in bed all afternoon. There was another patient in the room, in the bed closest to the door, who had company all afternoon. Sarah Baker couldn't have left the room without being seen."

"We were talking about the money aspect of it earlier," Shelley said.

"What money aspect?"

"Just speculating whether there was one," Jane said. "Stonecipher seemed to have a great deal of money — or at least to spend a lot. So anything having to do with the law firm's income might reflect on his wife, or Tony Belton, or Emma herself. You said you had people looking into that. Have they found anything?"

"Not yet. And it's a tricky legal situation."

"Why?" Jane asked.

"Because the firm belongs to Stonecipher and Belton. Stonecipher is dead, of natural causes. Belton isn't officially a suspect. Weyrich was merely an employee who was killed in her own apartment outside office hours. There are all sorts of privacy considerations that have to be danced around very carefully. If Mrs. Stonecipher and Tony Belton voluntarily opened the books and tax records and such, it would be a different story."

"But they're refusing?" Shelley asked, her eyes going a bit slitty.

"Not exactly refusing. Waffling. Delaying. Asking more questions than they're answering. And to be honest, there's nothing inherently suspicious about that. You and your husband wouldn't fling information about your business into the lap of the police if one of your employees was murdered, would you?"

"No, but we wouldn't have anything to do with the murder, either," Shelley said indignantly.

"And maybe they don't," Mel said. "Besides, Stonecipher himself was only buried this morning. If his wife and partner have nothing to do with Emma's death, why would they bother to stop in the middle of funeral preparations to help us?"

"I hate it when you're so fair and reasonable!" Jane said.

"Don't kid yourself. You love it," he said with a grin. It was the first time he'd smiled since he arrived.

"Was Tony at the deli opening?" Shelley asked. "It seems so long ago already that I don't remember."

"It doesn't seem like he was until after Stonecipher died and Emma called him," Mel said. "Nobody mentioned seeing him there earlier and he said he was at the office."

"That should be easy to prove," Jane said.

"Not entirely, but it doesn't really matter. Weyrich and Stonecipher were gone and the secretary had a dental appointment. He was there by himself. But as I keep reminding you, nobody killed Stonecipher."

"But somebody pushed that rack over on him," Jane said. "Surely that's significant."

"Probably, but I can't figure out how," Mel said.

"You're positive it couldn't have been an accident? Somebody bumping against it without even knowing he was there? Or a leg of it collapsing under its own weight?"

"No way. Before we realized it was a natural death, it was set back up and tested. Even our heftiest officer, pretending to stumble into it, could only rock it slightly. And that was with the shelves empty. Loaded up, it would have been even heavier and more stable. No, somebody had to give it a hard, deliberate push."

"Could a woman have had the strength?" Shelley asked.

"Have you got someone in mind?" Mel asked.

"No, just wondering."

"Yes, a woman could have done it. It's not so much a question of strength or weight as leverage. If you'd run into it accidentally, you'd hit it with your hip or shoulder and maybe rattle a few small items off the shelves. But it's not nearly as hard to make it go over if you reach up and push with both hands."

"I guess the thing was thoroughly fingerprinted," Jane said.

"Of course. The Bakers' and Mrs. Axton's prints were all over it, which they should have been. And there were some smudges in the area where someone might have pushed it."

"You don't mean to suggest that somebody came to the deli opening expecting to find Robert Stonecipher dead, planned ahead to push the rack over on him, and brought gloves along for the purpose!" Shelley exclaimed.

"Say, that's a theory I hadn't considered," Mel said. "Sorry to be sarcastic. No, there were a good half dozen people handling the thing, trying to pull the rack off him just in case he might still be revived. They're the ones who smudged it up."

"Mel, this whole thing — someone pushing that rack onto his body — has to have a connection to Emma's death, doesn't it?" Jane asked.

He shrugged. "Frankly, your guess is as good as mine. I don't believe in coincidences, but I sure can't come up with any reasons that anybody would do it."

"Okay, let's really think about this," Jane said.

"You and Shelley think," Mel said. "I'm going to eat cookies and give my brain a break."

"Okay," Shelley said in her organizational voice. "Here's the situation: X finds Y dead on the floor —"

"Apparently dead," Jane interrupted.

"Good. Yes, that might make all the difference. X finds Y sprawled on the floor.

Maybe dead. Maybe unconscious. Pushes a heavy thing over on him, making it look like Y was murdered. So, what could the reasons be?"

"Sheer frustration," Jane said. "X hated Y, planned to kill him, and is furious to think somebody else got to it first and lashes out in a fit of pique."

"Okay, that's one," Shelley said. "Sheer hatred. X hated Y, but couldn't take any action against him, so when he sees him helpless for once, he's overcome by the impulse to dish out vengeance. And even if he knew for sure that Y was already dead, that hatred might just need the outlet of pretending to kill him."

"A bit more baroque," Jane said as if evaluating a painting. "How's this: X finds Y lying dead on the floor — doesn't necessarily even know or care who it is, but has a rabid hatred for Z —"

"Z?" Shelley asked indignantly.

"Let me finish. X hates Z and thinks by pushing the rack over on Y, he can blame it on Z."

"Who could Z be?" Shelley asked, still apparently resentful of the introduction of this new character.

"The first person who comes to mind is Conrad, just because it's his deli. Or maybe X planned to claim later that he'd seen Z leave the room just before the crash."

"If that were the case, why didn't X ever make such an accusation?" Shelley asked.

As serious as the subject really was, Jane felt a sense of ghoulish amusement take over. "Try this one then: X knows Y is having an affair with Z and was once married to Q, who is trying to haul him into court to testify in a drug-running case against P —"

"— and S knew all about it and was threatening to tell M, who feared that K would hear about it and All Would Be Revealed!" Shelley finished. "I like it, Jane. Mel, we've solved it. You can probably still make your arrest this evening if you hurry."

Mel stared at them and then spoke very slowly and deliberately. "I thank all that is holy that you two didn't go into law enforcement."

— 21 —

Jane couldn't sleep, which was a rare affliction for her. She claimed, only half joking, that anywhere that you could throw down a blanket and wad of something soft resembling a pillow was a good enough bed. She prided herself on being a champion sleeper, so on the rare occasions when she had insomnia, it made her furious. And that, naturally, made it worse.

She'd gone to bed not long after Shelley and Mel left and spent a luxurious hour finishing the Dorothy Sayers book she'd been reading in ten-minute bits since the week before. The rain had stopped, so she opened her bedroom window, turned out the light, and snuggled down to enjoy the cool air and, with any luck at all, dream about Lord Peter.

She was still flouncing around, trying out various comfortable positions, and waiting for sleep, when she heard Mike come in. She thought about calling good night to him in the hopes that he might feel like a chat, but rejected the idea. He'd think she'd waited up for him on purpose. Finally she nodded off, only to be awakened again at four-thirty when Max, who had positioned himself in the open bedroom window, saw a creature in the yard and gave a low, eerie growl.

Jane gave up.

She closed the window — it had gotten downright chilly — threw some sweats on over her nightgown, and decided she'd go downstairs and find another book to read. While she was at it, she'd get some laundry started while nobody was awake to complain about the washing machine interfering with showering. She gathered up an armload of dark clothes and crept quietly downstairs.

Max and Meow thought the whole thing was great. Night was their favorite time and there was so seldom anyone awake to enjoy it with them. They lashed themselves against her legs and made chirruping is-it-breakfast-time? noises. Jane dumped the dirty clothes by the basement door and opened a can of cat food, then picked the clothes up again and went down to throw them in the wash. She considered booting up the computer and playing a little solitaire while she was down there, but it was cold and vaguely clammy in the basement, and besides, she didn't want to think.

When she came back up, she got a glass of milk and sat down at the kitchen table. The room was a mess. She hadn't even loaded up the dishwasher after dinner, and the empty but crusty macaroni pan was still soaking in the sink. She'd at least scrub it out and get the nasty plates out of sight. Then she could really clean the kitchen in the morning.

But one thing led to another. Once she got the plates, glasses, and silverware off the counter and out of the sink, it was silly not to go ahead. She worked her way along the counter, tidying up. At the wall, where the phone was, there were a couple scraps of paper with phone numbers, which she tacked onto the little bulletin board. There was also a paper sack. She glanced into it and remembered that it was the trash sack from Mike's car that she'd tossed there when she came home the night before.

Jane headed for the wastebasket, then thought better of it. Shelley had said it was trash, but it might not all be. If Mike had some car gadget in the sack and she pitched it, she'd be in trouble. She threw away the items in it one by one. Gum wrappers, a wadded-up empty cigarette pack, a couple of receipts from the deli, a yellowed newspaper clipping —

Jane had thrown away the clipping before she realized there was a familiar name on it. She pulled it back out, set it on the counter, and read it.

Then read it again.

"Mel, I'm sorry. Did I wake you?" she asked.

His voice over the phone was blurry and irritable. "Janey, it's seven in the morning. Of course you woke me up!"

"You got off lucky. I've been waiting to call for two hours."

"What's wrong?"

"Nothing's wrong, but I think I've got the solution. I've been thinking about it for hours and it all fits. There was a clipping — well, I won't explain it now, but can you come over?"

"Now?"

"Not right now. I guess there's not that much of a rush, but there are things you're going to need to check on."

"I'll be there by eight."

Despite her lack of sleep, Jane was wide awake. She ran down to the basement to throw the laundry into the dryer, thinking that by the time she'd showered, her jeans would be dry. As she came back up this time, she noticed a spot of color on the floor at the top of the steps. She picked up the little blue lozenge of paper that must have fallen out of her jeans pocket.

Nodding, she picked it up and said aloud, "Yes! Yes, it was a green one that I saw. And that fits, too."

Mel arrived at eight, just as Shelley had gone out to pick up her newspaper. She flung the paper in her kitchen door and followed him to Jane's.

"What's going on?" Shelley demanded when Jane ushered them in.

"I've got it," Jane said. "It was in that trash sack in Mike's car. Look!" She showed them the clipping on the kitchen counter. "I'm sorry. I touched it, but when I realized what it was I didn't touch it again. There might be fingerprints!"

Mel and Shelley leaned over together and read. Then Mel said, "Jane, is Mike up yet?"

"He'll be down in a minute. I woke him when I saw you drive up."

Shelley was still studying the clipping. "But Jane, this must mean —"

"I'm afraid it does."

Mike staggered into the kitchen, rumpled and grouchy. "Mom, what in the world — oh, Mel. Mrs. Nowack."

"Mike, I need to ask you about the trash sack that was in your car," Mel said.

"Trash? Oh, yeah. What about it?"

"Where did you pick it up and when?"

"At the deli," he said, rubbing his eyes. "Saturday morning, I think. Yeah, Saturday when I went in to work. There was junk people had dropped along the sidewalk and I had the paper bag in my car from buying some batteries, so I just picked up some of the junk."

"The front sidewalk?" Mel asked. "Did anyone see you doing that?"

"I don't know. It was no big deal."

"Mike, look at this newspaper clipping, but don't touch it," Mel said. "Is this part of what you picked up?"

Mike glanced at it. "I guess so. I'm sorry, but it was just trash. I didn't really look at it, I just picked it up and put it in the bag."

"Thanks, Mike. Go back to bed," Mel said as he picked the clipping up with tweezers and carefully put it in a plastic bag.

"What now?" Jane asked.

"Now you two keep very quiet and let me get to work. I'll call you later," Mel said. "For God's sake, don't talk to anybody about this. No more snooping! Understand?"

When he'd gone, Jane suddenly felt exhausted. Her frenzied, largely sleepless night suddenly caught up with her.

"What's wrong?" Shelley asked as Jane sat down at the kitchen table.

"I was up half the night. I fried my brain thinking about this."

"Then go back to bed. There's nothing more we can — or should — do."

"Don't you want to know —"

"Sure, but I think I see the general outline. I'll come back and blast you out at noon if I haven't heard from you sooner."

Jane dragged herself upstairs and fell, still dressed, into bed. She woke up again in what seemed like a couple minutes, but was actually nearly four hours. She was sitting on the patio drinking a cola and smoking a cigarette when Shelley found her. "I take it you haven't heard from Mel yet?" Shelley asked.

"Not a peep."

"I have a dental appointment in a few minutes, then I have to go to the library. Say about two-thirty? Want to go along?"

Neither of them mentioned what was uppermost in her mind.

"That sounds fine," Jane said.

Shelley tooted her horn on the dot of half past two. In the meantime, Jane had cleaned her basement office and found two more overdue library books.

"They'll send the library police for you if you keep doing that," Shelley said with a strained smile. "Mike's not working today, is he?"

"No. Let me turn these in and pay my fines, then we'll talk."

As they entered the library, a familiar figure was standing at the pay phone by the door. "Oh, Jane! Shelley!" Grace Axton said, hanging up. "I was trying to call you two. Conrad's got another artichoke thing he wants you to test." She indicated the books she was holding under one arm. "Then he's moving into raspberries since they're the currently trendy fruit. What's wrong?"

"Nothing," Jane and Shelley said in unison, then laughed nervously.

"Are you just returning those books?" Grace asked.

"And picking up a couple I had on reserve," Shelley said.

"Okay, I'll wait with you," Grace said. "The raspberries were Sarah's idea," she said happily as Shelley and Jane conducted their business. "She's starting to take more of an interest in the food. I'm starting to wonder if maybe Conrad was right that she was overly tired. Since she's been back from the hospital, I really think there's been a change. Not much. Very subtle. But I don't think I'm imagining it."

Grace continued to chat as they went back out to their cars. Once under way, Jane said to Shelley, "I don't like this. If Mel sees my car at the deli, he'll think we're snooping or gossiping."

"We'll be in and out so fast there won't be a chance," Shelley said. "I've just remembered an appointment that will make us have to run through."

"I'm parking in back, just in case," Jane said. They followed Grace's car through the alley behind the deli and as they were pulling in to the small parking area, another car came right behind them. Patsy Mallett got out, already talking. "I've been trailing you and honking for three blocks!" she said. "You two must really be preoccupied. I've got some of those food order records I promised to copy for you, Shelley. I was going to drop them in your mailbox, but I saw you pull out of the library and thought — hi, Grace. Were you in front of them? What a parade!"

"We're testing another recipe," Grace said. "Come join us."

"Worse and worse," Shelley whispered to Jane.

Conrad greeted them effusively. "Perfect timing! I just took them out of the oven. Wait until you see these, ladies."

He escorted them through the kitchen, past the deli cases, and to the seating area, empty now that the lunch hour was well past. Sarah trailed along behind with plates and silverware. Grace brought up the rear with a tray of glasses and a pitcher of iced tea. When they were all settled, Conrad came out with a casserole dish and removed the lid with a flourish. Inside were a half dozen large artichokes, hollowed out and filled with a rich stuffing. They were topped with browned Parmesan cheese with herbs mixed in. The smell was heavenly.

With great formality he placed one on each plate. He was just sitting down himself when the front door opened. Mel VanDyne and two uniformed officers came in. Mel looked over the group at the table and glared for a long moment directly at Jane.

"Hello? We're not open for meals right now," Conrad said. "But if you'd like to come back at five —"

Mel said, "Conrad Baker, I'm arresting you for the murder of Emma Weyrich —"

Conrad stood up, his face darkening.

"Sarah, go upstairs," he said in a low, fierce tone.

She stood automatically and started to walk away, then turned and said, very calmly, "No, Conrad."

Mel was reciting the Miranda warning. "Do you understand?" he finished.

"Yes, yes. But this is all a mistake. You can't arrest me. I haven't done anything. Sarah, I said to go upstairs!"

He started to move toward her, and the larger of the uniformed officers glided into his path and took his arm. "No, sir. You're coming with us."

Grace had gotten up from the table and gone to Sarah. Jane, afraid to meet Mel's disapproving gaze, looked at them instead. Sarah seemed suddenly taller. Sturdier. And for the first time, Jane could see a resemblance between the sisters.

— 22 —

The next four hours were hectic. Mel and one officer took Conrad away. Sarah and Grace were asked to come along in the second police car for questioning.

Grace looked as if she'd been hit in the stomach. "Ladies, I'm going to have to lock up," she said tentatively.

Patsy, ever practical, asked, "Who's going to cook dinner? Surely you have orders to fill and people will be coming to eat here in another two hours."

"We'll just have to close down for the day," Grace said. "Probably close down entirely."

"No!" Sarah said firmly. "No, we're not closing. This is ours, Grace — yours and mine — and we're not crumpling up and throwing it away as if it's nothing!"

Jane, Shelley, Patsy, and Grace all stared at Sarah as if she'd suddenly turned into an alien life form.

Shelley was the first to recover. "Then we'll stay and take care of things. The recipes are written down somewhere, aren't they? Jane, you call Mike and get him in here to help us find everything. Patsy, report to your family what's become of you and then call mine, too, if you don't mind."

Grace was the one looking confused and fragile for a change. "Conrad? Conrad killed that woman? But why? I don't understand."

"I'll tell you all about it, Grace," Sarah said. "There's all the time in the world now." Suddenly her shoulders started shaking and she put her face in her hands, sobbing, "Oh, God! I'm free."

Shelley, in brisk mode, said, "Grace, we'll take care of everything here. Don't forget your purse. Here it is. Go along now."

The second officer escorted them out the front door. Patsy looked at Jane. "I don't understand any of this!"

"I'll explain —" Jane began.

"Jane!" Shelley called over her shoulder as she headed for the kitchen, walking hard on her heels. "Have you made your phone call yet? There's no time for talk now. We have to fix dinner for about fifty people. Patsy, with all due respect, you aren't allowed near the food preparation."

"I waitressed all through college. I carry plates very well. Maybe I'll get one of my daughters to hunt in the attic for my old fishnet stockings and short skirt." They all burst into laughter at this idea.

They concocted a flimsy story about Grace, Sarah, and Conrad being called away suddenly on a family matter, and cut the menu in half, eliminating the more difficult dishes. Mike came through like a trouper, calling in another friend to help Scott with the deliveries while Mike himself took all the carry-out orders, packed them, and assigned delivery routes. Patsy's waitressing skills came back to her "like riding a bicycle," as she said. Shelley did the cooking and Jane got stuck with the dishwashing and vegetable peeling.

"Lot of good it does me to be the boss's best friend," she grumbled.

By seven-thirty, they'd locked the door behind the last diners and collapsed around the small kitchen table to eat leftovers. Mike excused himself with dire remarks about having to work on his day off and how he expected to be paid at least double. The women agreed that he'd been well worth double his salary, whatever it might be.

"So what is all this about!" Patsy said.

Jane washed down the last of her sandwich with a big gulp of coffee. "It all came together when I went through the trash from Mike's car," she said. "He'd come in to work Saturday and picked up stuff from the front side walk. Among other things there was an old newspaper clipping. About Sarah and Conrad's baby. I don't remember the exact wording, but the gist of the article was the background of the child's accident, his terrible affliction, and the fact that the parents wanted the life support removed. The local judge had been assumed to be sympathetic to that philosophy, but word had gotten out in the community and a citizens' group had been formed to protest any such judgment. The article mentioned that the citizens' group had been put together and was headed by 'local attorney and civic activist' Robert Stonecipher."

Patsy put her hands to her cheeks. "No! Oh, no! He was the one responsible for pressuring the judge to keep the baby alive!"

Jane nodded.

"But Conrad didn't kill Stonecipher. Nobody did."

"But at the time Emma died, neither Emma nor Conrad knew that," Jane said.

"Apparently Emma came over here Friday night after the high school graduation and waved that article around in Conrad's face, claiming that he had the best motive for killing Stonecipher and demanding money to keep quiet about it. Conrad must have been horrified," Jane said. "Not only was Emma threatening to put him in danger of arrest, but the whole ugly, upsetting story about the baby's death would become public in the town where they finally intended to settle."

Patsy nodded. "I can see his fear of the story about the baby getting out, but that alone wouldn't be worth killing someone for. And even the threat of arrest — well, Conrad knew he didn't kill Stonecipher because nobody killed him. I'm getting more confused. Did Conrad push the rack over on Stonecipher?"

"Yes," Jane said.

"But why make it look like murder?"

"That's what we all wondered, but we were looking at it backward," Jane said. "We kept saying, 'Why would anyone want an accident to look like murder?' when the truth was, Conrad probably thought it *was* murder and was trying to make it look like an accident."

"Who did he — ? Sarah? He thought

Sarah murdered Stonecipher?" Patsy said.

"That's my guess. Grace said Conrad was fanatic about not letting the local paper anywhere near Sarah. He was probably afraid she'd see Stonecipher's name in connection with some of his many causes and recognize it. As much as it upset him, think how much more it would upset her. But for all his efforts, he finds Stonecipher dead right there on the floor of the storage room and probably leaped to the conclusion that Sarah had identified him, gone berserk, and killed him. So he tried to make it look like an accident. Conrad's a big, tall man and didn't realize that just reaching out and shoving the rack over wasn't going to be that easy, even for him, and certainly not for a smaller person."

They heard the front door open and fell silent. Grace and Sarah were talking quietly as they moved toward the stairs. As their steps died away, Patsy said, "What was the article doing — wherever you said Mike found it?"

Shelley said, "The police had a witness who saw Emma going out Friday night in her jogging clothes, but carrying car keys and a file folder. It must have been the folder containing the article. It probably wasn't one of the blackmail files. I'd guess it was a sort of clipping file Stonecipher kept on himself. Mentions of him in newspapers and such. She was certainly bright enough to have made a copy or at least a notation of the paper and date."

Jane took up the story. "She must have given Conrad the clipping, which he subsequently dropped. When he discovered that it was missing, he was frantic. Grace told me they'd had trouble with raccoons emptying the trash cans all over the place Sunday night."

Patsy nodded. "Conrad rummaging for the missing clipping."

"Right," Jane said. "And when he didn't find it, he remembered that Mike had tidied up the yard. So he looked in Mike's car while it was parked in back and Mike was working inside the deli. Mike told me someone had been in his car, but hadn't taken anything. Conrad again."

"But Jane, all of this is what *could* have happened. Where's the proof of any of it? The police don't recklessly arrest people who might have a reason to murder someone."

Jane looked uncomfortable. "I haven't talked to Mel since early this morning. They obviously have physical evidence to support the theory or they wouldn't have arrested Conrad. Maybe both his and Emma's fingerprints were on the clipping in spite of it having been mauled around. And there was the paper dot from the folders."

She explained briefly to Patsy about the little paper lozenges. "When he showed me one, I knew I'd seen such a thing before. I think — yes, I have it here." She had put the blue dot back in her jeans pocket and now placed it on the kitchen table.

Patsy stared at it for a minute. "Hmm. Looks familiar in a way —"

"You and I saw a green one. At the same time."

Patsy dosed her eyes for a moment, then opened them very wide. "Stuck in the treads in the bottom of Conrad's sneaker when I ran into you here! I thought it was an odd-colored piece of grass."

"The deep treads in his sneakers picked it up from the carpet in her apartment."

"So he met her Friday night — ?"

"I think he not only met her," Jane said, "I think she made the poor guy jog around the block with her while she laid out her threats. Remember, Conrad had his shoe off because he had a blister on his heel. They were old sneakers. He wouldn't get a blister from any normal activity. It would have really added insult to injury to make him trot alongside her like a pet dog."

"And he went to her apartment Saturday to kill her?"

"I don't know. Maybe she'd told him to bring money and he went to do that, but saw the other folders and realized she was making several other people's lives a misery and simply lost control."

"He didn't take a weapon along," Shelley said. "She was killed with one of those hand weights from her own apartment."

"Did he take the rest of the folders?" Patsy asked, then said, "He must have. But if he did, where are they?"

Jane shrugged. "Maybe the police found them. Maybe they're still in his car. If it had been me, I'd have gone by the nearest fast food restaurant and pitched them in the Dumpster or a trash barrel."

Shelley got up and started clearing the table.

"To think — he did it all out of love for Sarah," Patsy said.

"No, he didn't," Grace said from the doorway.

They hadn't heard her approach.

"I wasn't deliberately eavesdropping," she said. "Just standing there for a minute working up the courage and energy to face you all."

Jane pulled out a chair and gestured for Grace to sit down. She did so wearily. She looked like a soldier returning from a long, exhausting battle — but a victorious one. "Don't waste your good thoughts on Conrad," she said finally.

"You don't have to tell us anything, Grace, but we're here to listen if you'd like to talk," Patsy said.

Grace smiled. "I know you are. Conrad didn't kill that woman out of love of Sarah. Out of need for control, revenge, money — but not love. The police only questioned us for a short time this afternoon and told us they'd be back tomorrow morning. The rest of the time you dear ladies were doing our jobs, Sarah and I were sitting in the car talking. We got years' worth of talk into a few hours. Or at least Sarah did. Shelley, could I ask you for one more — ? Oh, thank you. You read my mind."

She took a long drink from the glass of iced tea Shelley had handed her, organized her thoughts for a moment, and said, "It's terribly complex and I don't know if I can sum it up, but Conrad blamed Sarah for the baby's death. And why not? She blamed herself. He told her that it was only fitting that she should have to face him — the child's father — every day of her life. She was so consumed by guilt that it seemed a fitting punishment to her. A way to atone, I guess. After she'd been out of the mental hospital for a while, he never mentioned it again. He was always terribly kind to her. Very protective. She had no friends, no life of her own, no part in any community, but she felt she had no right to complain. Every time they moved to a new place, he'd make all the more sure she was dependent on him. If she started making friends, rumors would start about her and people would turn away — often in disgust. She knew he was responsible, but could never absolutely prove it, not even to her own satisfaction."

"How horrible!" Patsy whispered.

"And then they came back here," Shelley said.

Grace nodded. "Torturing her must have become a bit boring and he was attracted to the idea of having a business and being 'somebody.' Especially since it didn't cost him anything."

"What do you mean?" Jane asked.

"I made sure our grandmother left the house jointly to me and Sarah. She and I mortgaged it and used the cash to fund the business. He liked the idea of not having to put any money in, but didn't grasp at first that it belonged, lock, stock, and barrel, to Sarah and me. But Sarah knew it. And it finally gave her some power over her own life."

"But she didn't act like it," Jane said. "She was so shy and remote, even with you."

"Especially with me," Grace said. "She was afraid to show her hand for fear he'd somehow turn me against her, just like he had everyone else. She intended to tell me all this once the deli opened and business was under way, but then . . ." She paused, swallowing back a sob.

"— Stonecipher died," Shelley finished briskly. "And she went to pieces. Why?"

"Because she thought Conrad had killed him as some kind of warning to her. She had no idea who Stonecipher was and neither did I. When the baby was dying, Sarah and I just concentrated on him and each other and didn't read the newspapers. Then Conrad visited her at the hospital the other day and started telling her she'd killed Stonecipher, but he'd covered it up and made it look like an accident."

Patsy stood up suddenly and paced the kitchen. "This is so terrible I can hardly stand to hear it! I'm so angry I could —"

Grace got up and put an arm around her old friend. "Calm down, Patsy. It didn't work. Sarah's not stupid or crazy. She saw through him. He either believed she'd killed the man, which showed an intolerable failure to understand her at all, or he was trying to make her believe she was a murderer, which insulted her considerable intelligence. It's a good thing he did it, really. That was what finally made her fully realize how wicked he was."

"What did he tell her about Emma's death?" Jane asked. "Or did he try to keep it a secret."

"He told her the truth — or at least part of it," Sarah said. "That Emma had threatened to expose that Sarah had, through her own carelessness, killed their child. And that he had killed Emma to 'protect' Sarah. Conrad was supposed to be taking next weekend off to attend a seminar in Detroit on commercial cooking techniques. Sarah was going to wait until he was gone, then tell me and the police everything."

"So he killed Emma to keep her from telling everyone why the baby died?" Shelley said. "But he'd spread the same rumor himself."

"Only when and where he wanted to. When it turned people away from Sarah," Grace said. "Coming here was different. He wanted to stay here. He wanted them both to be well-liked. He wanted, in short, to get rich and comfortable on Sarah's and my inheritance. And he had to keep that threat to himself, to hold over her. But that's not the main reason he killed Emma, I don't think. You have to remember that when she was killed, nobody knew Stonecipher had died of a heart attack. Emma must have showed him the clipping, made a good case for him being suspected of Stonecipher's murder. And for all Conrad knew then, he might have actually killed Stonecipher."

"What do you mean?" Shelley asked.

Grace sighed. "He came into the storeroom and saw Stonecipher lying there looking dead. He apparently leaped to the conclusion that Sarah really had gone mad and had killed the man. So, in the heat of the moment, he tried to make it look like an accident. But it had to have crossed his mind later that Stonecipher might have only been unconscious and that he himself *had* killed him by pushing the rack over. And all the time he was acting like the perfect husband, protecting his poor frail, crazy wife. And looking like a saint the whole time."

"You had a phrase for that, Patsy," Jane said.

"I did?"

"Yes, you called it deadly kindness. Remember?"

When Shelley and Jane finally started home, Shelley said, "They're going to need a new cook. Grace said Conrad had hired an assistant who's supposed to start tomorrow, but they'll have to hire someone to replace Conrad. I was thinking about volunteering to fill in for a few days until they can hire a professional. I have to admit that I enjoyed being the chef du jour."

Jane thought for a minute. "I recently gave Katie a rather pompous lecture about helping the world by starting in your own neighborhood. I guess I could waitress for a couple days to free Grace to interview and hire a cook. Uh-ho!" Jane added as she pulled into the driveway and saw Mel's car approaching. "I've got some explaining to do. He was furious that we were at the deli when he came to arrest Conrad."

"You'll manage," Shelley said. "Just be very, very kind," she added with a wicked laugh.

— About the Author —

Jill Churchill is the bestselling author of the Jane Jeffry mystery series for Avon Books. The first in the series was nominated as "Best First Novel" for the Anthony award and won both the prestigious Agatha and the Macavity awards in the same category. She says writing this series is the best treat she can have without a knife and fork.

Under her real name, Janice Young Brooks is an avid amateur genealogist. Like her sleuth, she lives in midwestern suburbia, but without half of Jane Jeffry's murderous adventures.

The employees of Thorndike Press hope you have enjoyed this Large Print book. All our Thorndike and Wheeler Large Print titles are designed for easy reading, and all our books are made to last. Other Thorndike Press Large Print books are available at your library, through selected bookstores, or directly from us.

For information about titles, please call:

(800) 223-1244

or visit our Web site at:

www.gale.com/thorndike
www.gale.com/wheeler

To share your comments, please write:

Publisher
Thorndike Press
295 Kennedy Memorial Drive
Waterville, ME 04901